The Wooden Box and Other Stories

By Michael J. Lowis

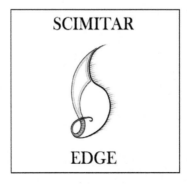

SCIMITAR

EDGE

Published by Scimitar Edge

An imprint of Purple Unicorn Media

ISBN 978-1-915692-35-1

Cover design by Steven Phillips

Also by Michael J. Lowis

The Gospel Miracles: What Really Happened? (2014)

Euthanasia, Suicide, and Despair: Can the Bible Help? (2015)

Ageing Disgracefully, With Grace (2016)

Twenty Years in South Africa: An Immigrant's Tale (2017)

What Do We Know About God? Evidence from the Hebrew Scriptures (2017)

Reincarnation: An Historical Novel Spanning 4,000 Years (2018)

From the Pope to Pigeons; from Dreams to Heaven: Twenty Essays & Anecdotes (2018)

What's it all about, then? Observation on life and the changing times (2019)

Two Mikes and their 39 stories (2020) (as co-author)

Djoser and the Gods (2022)

The Pharaoh and the Shabti (2022)

Contents

The Wooden Box
And Other Stories

The Wooden Box

"Mummy, why does Grandma Louise keep pointing to that fancy wooden box on the sideboard and saying that I should ask *him*, when I ask her a question she can't answer?"

Mary didn't respond straight away. She knew what the answer was, but hesitated to tell Sophie the truth. Her eight-year-old daughter had reached that perceptive age when children start to query one thing after another. Although she always tried to give the correct answers, there were times when she decided it might be best to shield immature minds from some of the harsher realities of life. After all, there'd be plenty of opportunities during the next few years to gently introduce her to some of the less pleasant realities most of us will have to face.

"Oh, it's just Grandma's way of saying that she doesn't know, darling," Mary replied, adding, "Perhaps there's a magic genie in the box that knows the answers to everything but doesn't want to reveal them just yet." This seemed to satisfy Sophie for the time being. As her daughter scampered off to play with her younger brother, Charlie, the memory of events that led up to the origin of that special box came drifting back into her mother's mind.

Mary had spent her early childhood living in Africa. Her younger sister, Margaret, was born out there. Father Tom was a microbiologist, funded by the British Medical Research Council to carry out a long-term study on tropical diseases. When not caring for the two children, her mother Louise devoted her spare time to charity work, and especially to the education of children living in the rural areas where schools were virtually non-existent.

It was a pleasant life, away from harsh winters of England and the seemingly endless industrial disputes there that invariably ended in strikes. Yes, it did sometimes become just a bit too hot and, during the dry season, you had to be careful not to waste a single drop of precious water. But the fresh air, open spaces, and visits to the game reserves made it all worthwhile.

Sometimes, during the school holidays, both she and Margaret were able to accompany their father on his field trips to the more remote villages, leaving their mother free of family responsibilities and able to devote more time to her voluntary work. Shortly after Mary's thirteenth birthday Tom announced that he needed to make one of these excursions, and asked the girls if they would like to join him. "Yes please," they responded in unison, but none of them could have known that this would be the last one they would make together.

Next day, after collecting the equipment they'd need to camp out in the bush, they squeezed it into the back of their four-wheel-drive vehicle. After a two-hour journey over unmade roads, they erected the large tent they would share and the girls then unpacked the camp beds and portable cooking stove. Tom tried never to leave his daughters alone, being aware of potential intrusions by both the animals and the less savoury members that populate any society. If he had to be away from the camp for any length of time, he always left the two-way radio with them so they could contact the regional office in an emergency.

From as far back as she could remember, Mary had loved music, and always delighted in the sound of African singing. She marvelled at the way one member of a group could strike up a melody, and immediately the others joined in, sometimes in harmony. It was a gift she wished she had herself. Not only was it harmonious, but it was also emotional, usually more sad than happy. But there was another emotion that invaded the music on certain occasions, which she was to experience sooner than she could have anticipated.

"Daddy, why don't we organise a choir competition between members of different villages?" Mary asked during breakfast the next morning. "I'm sure everyone would enjoy this, and we certainly would."

Tom considered this for a few moments before replying. It would mean bringing members from different villages together in one place. In the past there had been skirmishes and disagreements between the various communities, especially when competing for game during hunting trips. Would such an event help to bring about future cooperation, or would it just exacerbate the rivalry? "It's a great idea, Mary," he eventually replied. "But it might not be as easy to organise as you think. I'll have a word with the local chief to see what he has to say."

Mary still remembered how, all those years ago, she had tried to keep herself busy tidying up the tent and chatting to Margaret. Once she'd entered the era of the teenager, she took pride in adopting the role of homemaker when they were away from their mother. But it was hard for her to remain calm when she was impatient to hear what her father had to say when he came back from his meeting.

It was lunchtime before Tom at last returned. "Sorry it's taken so long, Mary, but the Chief didn't want to give me an answer before consulting with the tribal elders. I just carried on with my work and then went back to see him a few minutes ago."

"And what did he say?" Mary asked, unable to wait any longer.

"He's agreed, and will send messengers to the heads of the surrounding villages. But he shares our concerns that what is meant to be a friendly competition may end up being a battle."

Mary gave a big smile. "Thank you, daddy. I'm still glad the Chief agreed, and we must just try to keep it all friendly."

"Of course we must," her father said. "We can hope that a peaceful contest like this will encourage the different villagers to cooperate in more important ways such as sharing food and water, and helping each other when there's illness or a fire."

"Or even providing a school for all the children in the area," added Mary.

For the girls, it was like waiting impatiently for Christmas, but the day of the choir contest finally dawned and the contestants from the villages started to arrive. "Daddy, why are the men dressed in warrior outfits and carrying assegai spears and shields?" Mary asked, a puzzled expression replacing her usual smile.

"Don't worry about this," Tom assured his daughters, seeing the consternation on their faces. "They bring these weapons with them so they can beat them together to add rhythm to their singing."

Everyone assembled around a large area in the middle of the village. At one side a goat had been slaughtered and was being roasted on an open fire. Mary noticed there were several buckets of liquid placed nearby, and some of the men dipped beakers into them and drank the contents. "What are they drinking?" she asked her father.

"That's the local beer," he replied. "They buy a powder from the local store, tip into a bucket overnight, and it's ready the next day. I tried it once but it was too rough for me."

It was the ladies who gave their performances first, all dressed in their traditional colourful robes. Mary was delighted to once again hear those wonderful, spontaneous harmonies, steeped in emotion, which just seemed to flow naturally. What a pity she couldn't understand the words, but it sounded to her as if these were religious offerings, maybe lamenting hardships from the past and hopes for better things to come. Everyone was well behaved, and applauded each other with their customary raised hands and whoops of appreciation.

Next came the men. The group from the home village marched into the area in single file, chanting, stamping their feet and banging their assegais against the shields to a rhythmic beat. Feeling the need for protection, little Margaret moved closer to Tom and her elder sister. "They seem pretty warlike," Mary said to her father, sensing the aggression in the men's actions.

"Oh, I wouldn't worry about it," he replied. "These dances are just like play acting; they're substitutes for the real thing, or sometimes recreations of past conquests. Things are more civilised these days."

The warriors formed a circle, and their shouting, stamping and banging continued with even greater energy. Eventually the performance ended and they marched away to enthusiastic applause from their supporters. A group from the next village entered. It was clear from the onset they were intent on demonstrating even more aggression then had their opponents, and they also had had more time to imbibe the beer. Their shouting, stamping and waving of weapons was carried out with frantic vigour, before they also eventually made their exit.

Despite enjoying the singing earlier by the ladies, Mary was starting to doubt if this competition was a good idea. With her younger sister clinging to her for reassurance, she said, "Daddy, how many more groups are there to perform?"

"This is the last one," Tom answered, as a very wild-looking stream of warriors entered the area. "Our chief invited more, but only two of them agreed to come."

This group were spoiling for a fight. No doubt fortified by generous quantities of the home brew. The rivalry that was normally kept under control now burst through unchecked. After a brief but frenzied dance, the leader started shouting aggressively at the other performers. Although Mary had only picked up a few words of the local tongue, it was obvious he was mocking the other competitors, and challenging them to a confrontation.

Unable to resist, some of the other warriors responded by entering the area and hurling insults at their opponents. Tom was now starting to become concerned himself, and decided to intervene. "You go back to the vehicle and lock yourself inside," he said to his two daughters. "I'm going to try and calm things down a bit."

Despite Mary's plea for him to just leave the warring factions to it, their father walked into the middle of the group and held up his hands. "Please calm down, my friends," he said in a loud voice. "This is a peaceful and friendly competition. You are all winners, so why don't we all go and enjoy the food that's been prepared for us."

The girls were half way back to the car, but then turned round to see their father surrounded by warriors who were shouting and menacingly waving their spears. Suddenly he fell, clutching his right shoulder. They immediately ran back and straight into the arena. The sight of their wounded visitor caused the men to retreat far enough for his daughters to pass unhindered.

"Daddy, daddy," Mary screamed. "You've been hurt."

Tom held a handkerchief against his shoulder to try and staunch the blood flow. Attempting a smile he said, "Don't worry, I'll be alright. Let's just get to the vehicle together. There's a first aid kit there to bandage the assegai wound."

With an effort, Mary and Margaret helped their father to his feet, and carefully managed to walk him back to the car. Tom was clearly suffering, but a large swab secured tightly with strips of plaster did control the bleeding for the moment. Once this was done, he reached for the two-way radio and relayed the situation to the duty operator at the regional office. "Are you able to drive?" the official asked.

"I think so, but it's a two-hour, bumpy journey so I'm not sure how far I'll get," he replied.

"Well you set off, and we'll send an ambulance with a spare driver to meet you half way."

"Daddy, what about the tent and all the equipment we've left in it?" Mary said, as her father started the car and slowly drove away with just one hand on the steering wheel."

"Those can be replaced, but you two can not," he answered. "I need to get you safely away from this dangerous place."

They drove on, but it was clear that Tom was in pain and gradually weakening. "I'm so sorry I asked you to arrange the music competition," Mary said, trying to hold back the tears. "All this trouble only happened because of me."

"Please don't think that," her father replied gently. "It was a good idea, and it could have helped relationships rather than made them worse," he added, his voice starting to weaken.

They continued in silence, but after another half an hour Tom managed to stop the car just before he lapsed into unconsciousness.

Margaret was sobbing and obviously frightened. "What are we going to do? Is daddy going to die?"

Mary realised she had to take control, and cuddled her little sister. "Don't cry, Margaret, the ambulance from the office will be here soon, and I'm sure they'll take good care of daddy."

* * *

The noise of Sophie and Charlie running back into the house hoping for a chocolate biscuit suddenly brought Mary back to the present day. "Just run along and play for a few more minutes," she said. "I'll bring some milk and biscuits out to you soon."

As she walked into the kitchen, the memory of that fateful day remained with her. Yes, the ambulance did arrive mercifully soon afterwards, and the medics carefully lifted her father into it. The spare driver took the girls home to their mother, Louise, in their own four-wheel car.

Although Tom recovered from his wound, the assegai point had been dipped in poison similar to that obtained from the foxglove plant. It caused a weakness in his heart function. He never made any more field trips but continued working in the regional office for as long as he had the strength to do so.

Sadly, the disability brought about his death a year later. His body was cremated while they were still in Africa, and Louise had the ashes sealed inside the fancy wooden box that now resided on her sideboard back in England.

Mary wondered again if little Sophie was ready to hear the truth. Had her father still been here, he would no doubt have been able to answer many of the questions his granddaughter asked. But although he was not with them in person, his remains were, so perhaps her grandmother is right in just pointing to the wooden box and saying 'ask him'.

Alpha-Foxtrot-Bravo

Again, Jake pressed the microphone transmit button. "Mayday, Mayday, Mayday, this is alpha-foxtrot-bravo, come in please," he said, trying to mask the anxiety now starting to show in his voice. When he'd trained for his private pilot's licence, the instructor had repeatedly emphasised the need to avoid panicking during an emergency, as it could so easily interfere with a person's ability to think clearly.

His passenger, Millie, didn't share her boyfriend's apparent composure. "We're going to die, I know it," she cried out. "Why doesn't someone answer?"

The speaker continued to emit only the crackling sounds of radio static. "I'm sure they will soon," he replied, not altogether convincingly. "We're just over a hundred miles from Miami; if they can't hear us there then the control tower at Nassau should pick us up."

Jake was starting to wonder if it had been a good idea to join the syndicate of five college graduates who had decided to buy the twin-engine Cessna 310. The boys had met whilst studying at the University of Central Florida, and had joined the local flying club. He'd always been passionate about flying, and had jumped at the opportunity to take lessons and obtain a private pilot's licence.

Once they were qualified to fly, and their studies were over, the group remained in contact and agreed to share the cost of an affordable, second-hand aircraft. But being new graduates they had little money to spare. The fifteen-year-old, four-seater was budget price; despite its age it looked to be in good condition and had a certificate of airworthiness. The syndicate members had little hesitation in snapping it up.

They had drawn up a rota to ensure that each co-owner had equal opportunity to fly the plane, and it was now Jake's turn again. He was keen to impress his new girlfriend but Millie was initially reluctant to accept his invitation. She eventually succumbed to the young man's persistence. If only I'd not yielded and was now safe on terra firma, she lamented. But this was not the case – she was 8,000 feet up in the sky in a small, unreliable aircraft.

"The smoke pouring from the engine on the left is getting worse," Millie yelled. "You must do something."

"I'm trying to hold the aircraft steady," Jake replied, reaching for the microphone. "Mayday, Mayday, Mayday, this is alpha-foxtrot-bravo, fifty miles east of Nassau. We have engine failure. If anyone can hear me, please respond."

Turning to Millie he said, "I'm using the distress frequency and I'm sure someone will hear us now that we're getting closer to The Bahamas."

A voice broke through the static coming from the speaker. "Alpha-foxtrot-bravo, this is Nassau control tower. What is your status?"

Millie burst into tears. With an effort, Jake managed to avoid doing the same, realising that tears of relief might be premature. Trying to keep his voice steady he responded, "Hello Nassau, this is alpha-foxtrot-bravo. Glad you picked up my call for help. I'm in a Cessna 310 with one passenger. The port engine is emitting smoke and losing power."

"Understood. What is your flight plan?"

"We left Miami at twelve-hundred hours on a course for Nassau where we would land, have lunch, and then return to base."

Jake's report was interrupted by Millie shouting, "I can now see flames coming from the engine; we're going to die!"

"I heard that," the air traffic controller said. "You're not showing on my radar screen yet; what is your current position?"

"After climbing to 8,000 feet we've been cruising for an hour. I estimate we're less than fifty miles from your airport. Normally it would take about twenty minutes to reach you, but I'm losing both height and speed due to the engine failure."

There was a pause before any response, and Jake assumed the controller was discussing options with other members of his team. Eventually the speaker sprang into life again. "Acknowledged, alpha-foxtrot-bravo. You've just appeared on our radar, so we can now track your progress. We shall ensure all emergency services are standing by. Please continue to report your status, and good luck."

Jake used all he had been taught to try and keep the aircraft level and maintain speed, but it was a losing battle. He looked at the instrument panel. "I see we're now down to 6,000 feet and still forty miles from the airport," he commented.

Knowing that Nassau Control was aware of their situation had a calming effect on Millie, but there was no escaping the danger they were in. She also realised that Jake needed all the support she could give him if they were to come through this situation alive. "Are we going to make it to the landing strip, or crash before we reach it?" she asked as calmly as she could.

"I'll do my best, but can't be sure; it'll be touch and go depending on whether or not I can maintain sufficient altitude," he replied. "I'm really sorry this has happened, Millie. It was meant to be a romantic day out, but my attempt to impress you has backfired."

She put her hand on his shoulder. "Just don't worry about that for the moment, Jake; once this is all over we can have all the romantic days out we want. Mind you, for me to accept an invitation to fly into the Bermuda Triangle was asking for trouble!" she said, trying to end with a laugh that didn't quite materialise.

"Don't believe all those stories about the Triangle, it's just a series of coincidences . . ."

He was interrupted by the radio. "Alpha-foxtrot-bravo, this is Nassau airport control. The emergency services have been alerted. Please report your status."

Jake pressed the transmit button. "We're losing altitude at an increasing rate. I've stepped up the power on the starboard engine, but it's now starting to overheat. You'll see from the radar that we're still twenty-five miles from the airport, and have dropped to 2,000 feet."

"Understood," the controller acknowledged. "We've been monitoring your situation and it appears unlikely you will reach the runway. Rather than risk crashing on a housing area, we request you set a course over the sea and approach Old Fort Bay from the north. If you're too low to continue to the airport, you must take your chance and come down in the sea."

"Will do; changing course now. We are now down to less than 1,000 feet. It'll be a close call."

"Acknowledged. Please keep the transmission open so we can remain in contact."

Jake quickly went through the emergency procedures he'd learned during his training, and Millie wisely allowed him to concentrate without distraction. They rounded the western peninsula and then turned south for the final approach to the airport. "I think we might just make the landing strip," he said, both to the controller and Millie.

But then disaster struck. The starboard engine shut down. With no power, the aircraft rapidly descended toward the ocean. He just had time to shout, "Brace yourself – we're going down!" before they hit the water with a massive jolt.

The cockpit rapidly started to fill with water. Jake released his seat belt and struggled vainly to open the side door. The water came up over his head and he felt himself losing consciousness.

* * *

"Let's pull him into the boat," the rescue captain instructed one of his crew members. "But he doesn't seem to be breathing." Millie then clambered aboard and immediately started to administer mouth to mouth resuscitation. "Is it working?" he asked.

"Not yet," she snapped.

Jake suddenly coughed and regurgitated a large quantity of water. He opened his eyes. The first thing he saw were the lips of his girlfriend, inches from his own. "What happened?" he spluttered.

"We crashed. I managed to open the door on my side and then dragged you clear just in time before the plane sank," she replied with a smile.

"Thank you for saving my life, Millie," he said weekly, and with just a hint of embarrassment. "But how were you able to do all this with the cockpit full of water?"

"Whilst you were playing with aeroplanes during your college years, I was in the university endurance swimming team winning trophies. I had no problem holding my breath until I could pull you to safety and keep you afloat until the boat arrived – fortunately very quickly."

"All right you two, it's a good job the control tower immediately ordered the launch of the life boat when they realised you were coming down," the Captain interjected. "We're now returning to our base at Love Beach, and I'll ask the doctor there to check you both out."

* * *

"You two were lucky to escape with just a few bruises," the doctor reported when they were safely back shore. "But I suggest you rest up for a day or two before returning to Miami."

"Thanks doc," Jake said, now much recovered. "But tell me, is Love Beach the real name for this place?"

"Indeed it is. It's one of the closest beaches to the airport."

Jake smiled and took Millie's hand. "Love Beach, hmm, maybe the Bermuda Triangle did us a favour after all!"

The Explorer's Report

Byamee stood up. It was his turn. "O Venerable Leader, may I present to you this report of my expedition to explore new worlds," he said, handing over a magnetic disc. The Leader inserted it into the reader and then sat back to listen to the account of what the explorer had to say.

* * *

I went alone to the blue planet that I later learned the local population calls Earth. It is a long way from our own world, but I was maintained in a cryostatic state until my capsule entered its solar system. When circulating the globe, I spotted a large island surrounded by water and steered toward the middle of it. There, standing proud on the flat terrain, was a large red mountain. I set a course and landed on top of it.

There was no sign of any intelligent life forms. I left the capsule and set up camp so I could take my time surveying this new territory. Looking into the far distance across the plain, I could just make out a range of red-rock domes in the distance to break the monotony.

Unlike our own planet, this one had only a single nearby star. When it dropped below the horizon, it was very dark and I could feel the cold. I had to go back inside the capsule to keep warm. Eventually the sun rose again, so I could emerge and plan my exploration.

I firstly walked around the top of this red mountain. It was largely barren, with just occasional clumps of green foliage growing from cracks in the rock. But then I came across pools of water that must have been filled by the rain, because there was no evidence of any spring to supply them. Inside several of them were small living creatures with rounded bodies and long tails. I picked some of them up, and they did no harm to me.

My next plan was to descend to the plain. Surely these primitive little aquatic animals were not the only form of life on this planet, and I needed to see if there was anything more advanced. I looked for a pathway that would lead me safely down. When I found such a route and looked along it, I was unprepared for what I saw.

There, in the distance coming up toward me, was a line of living creatures. Was I in danger? Would I be seen as a threat that must be eliminated immediately? All I could do was stand and watch as they came closer. When it was possible to distinguish more detail, it was clear they were bipeds, walking on two limbs just like we do, and they also had two forelimbs.

Although there appeared to be other features that suggested a similar evolution to our own species, I still did not know if they would be aggressive toward me. Assuming that creatures so advanced as those drawing ever closer must have a way of communicating, I quickly went to collect the universal translation unit from the capsule. When I returned, they had reached the top of the hill.

I could now see them clearly. Indeed they were not vastly different from us in appearance, although their head and facial features were not identical to ours. What should I do, I wondered: stand boldly where I was, or find myself some protection in case of an attack?

Holding the translator in front of me, I stood my ground but hoped that my stance did not appear threatening. To my surprise, when the group of six individuals reached me, they knelt down and silently bowed their heads. Trusting that my words would be understood I said, "Greetings, my name is Byamee. Please do stand up so that we can see each other."

The universal translator must have been working, because they immediately stood up, and the one who seemed to be leader started to speak. His skin was a dark brown colour, not light like ours. Although he also had two eyes, and a mouth where his voice came from, there was a protuberance in the middle of his face. On top of his head was a mass of short dark hair, and not a ring of spikes like we have.

"My Lord Byamee, my name is Dundalli, and I am the chief of our tribe. We are honoured that you have at last come to visit us."

"I am puzzled," I replied. "Why did you think I would come, and how did you know I was here?"

"My Lord, we have often given thanks to our creator god, and prayed that he would one day come down from his throne on high and visit us. We saw your chariot arrive in the sky and land on this mountain."

I was faced with a dilemma. Should I tell them I was just an explorer from another world far away, and risk them becoming angry, possibly even hostile? Or should I let them continue to believe I was their god, and be sure of being treated with respect? I concluded that it would be best to just avoid this question, at least for the moment, until some measure of trust had been formed between us.

"Dundalli, my desire is to learn more about your world and its people," I said. "I would be pleased if you could teach me about this place, and take me to where you live."

"We shall certainly do as you ask," he replied. "I know the wishes of my people will be rewarded when they can see you for themselves."

"Very well," I responded. "But first you must rest from your long journey up the mountain. Whilst we are sitting, you can tell me the name of this place."

They made themselves comfortable, glad to have the chance to pause for a while before making the downward journey.

This is the land of Australia," Dundalli began. "We are the Aboriginal people, and some of us came from the Torres Strait Islands to the north. Our ancestors journeyed to this country many thousands of years ago. This mountain is called Uluru, and from this day it will be sacred, the place where you, our god, came to visit us.

Again I resisted the temptation to say I was just a simple explorer from another planet. Instead I asked, "So do all the inhabitants of your land have the same appearance as yourselves?"

"My Lord, I have been told there are many languages and shades of skin colour in the world, but all people are formed much the same as we are."

"That is interesting, and perhaps I shall be able to meet some of these others whilst I am here. But are we ready to descend the mountain now?"

The party moved toward the path and I followed. As we walked, Dundalli pointed out several caves. He said these provided refuge for climbers when they were caught in a storm, and that others sometimes come to paint pictures on the walls.

When we finally reached the plain below, a large crowd of people were there waiting for us, waving and singing. They did not come close enough to touch, but stopped a few paces away from me and became silent. Just as Dundalli and his party had done when they reached the top of the mountain, they all knelt down and bowed their heads.

This time I understood why they had done this, and spoke into the translator. "Please stand up, and let us greet each other. I have come a long way to meet you."

Dundalli then called three individuals to come forward. "My Lord Byamee, may I present to you my wife Kirra, my son Calute, and daughter Yindi." Like all the others I had seen, their clothing was simple – a cloth around the waist for the men, and a longer garment for the women. Despite what I had just asked, they started to kneel down in front of me, but I gestured to them to remain upright.

"I am pleased to meet you," I said, trying to put them at their ease. "Would you all like to guide me around your settlement and show me where you live?"

We went to the chief's house first. It was an oblong hut made of wood, and the roof was covered with foliage. Some of the other dwellings were formed by bending lengths of cane into domes or ridges, and covering them with what I was told were palm leaves. There were people cooking outside on open fires.

I asked Dundalli what food they ate. "We are hunters," he said proudly, taking a long stick with a pointed end from his hut. "With these spears, and our bows and arrows, we kill the animals we find on our expeditions. Also, we gather plants that we find growing in the bush."

We came to a man sitting on the ground. He had a pot of brown liquid, and was painting pictures on flat pieces of stone. "This is our artist, Nemarluck," the chief explained. "He preserves images of our life on these tablets, and also the cave walls on Uluru, so that future generations will remember us."

Dundalli bent down and there was a brief conversation between the two men. Nemarluck then looked up at me and said, "My Lord, if you will allow me, I would like to paint two pictures of you. One will be for yourself, and the other will be for us to keep as a reminder of your visit."

"Of course," I replied, thinking this would take some time. But he worked quickly and only moments later gave me a small slab of stone adorned with a simple image.

I thanked him, and we were just about to continue our tour when shouts came from the crowd. A man, breathless from exertion, ran up to us. "My Chief," he blurted out, "The invaders are coming."

"How close are they?" Dundalli asked, now looking very much like the man in charge.

"My hunting party saw them. They were about two miles away, and we ran back as quickly as possible to warn you."

"Go and tell all the men of the village to arm themselves and be ready for the attack," the Chief ordered. "We must protect our creator god down to the last man if necessary."

The messenger ran off and Dundalli turned to me. "My Lord, these invading parties come from time to time, and we ourselves are sometimes the invaders. But I regret this has happened during your long-awaited visit to us. We cannot allow anything to happen to you."

"Perhaps the other tribe also saw my arrival, and now wish to capture me," I suggested. "If this is so, then I am responsible for the danger you and your people are now in. It would be best if I made my way back up the mountain as quickly as possible, and left this land."

"Regrettably I have to agree, My Lord. But I shall arrange for my deputy, Bussamarai, and five warriors to accompany you to the path, and then stand guard at the bottom in case the invaders try to follow you."

I bid a hasty farewell to Dundalli and his family, and then my small party set off as quickly as possible toward the mountain. We had almost reached it before we saw the invaders, and they were coming toward us. "I think we shall be at the path before them," I said to Bussamarai. "But that will leave you vulnerable if you remain at the base."

"If necessary we shall gladly sacrifice ourselves to save you," he answered. This was not what I wanted to hear, but there was no time to argue; we had arrived at the start of the path. The invaders had almost reached us and I was pushed onto the slope by the brave warriors. They then formed a barrier to prevent anyone following me.

"Let me stop and help you," I pleaded, but Bussamarai just told me to go up the hill as fast as I could. Reluctantly, I turned and ran along the path until exhaustion compelled me to stop for a few moments. Looking back, I saw my guards battling to hold back the enemy and stop them following me. Several men had fallen to the ground, and they appeared to be lifeless.

I continued upwards, eventually reaching the top of the mountain. Once inside my capsule I knew I was safe, but was devastated to think that some of those I came to visit had probably lost their lives because of me. I piloted the capsule down to where the men were still fighting, and made as much noise as possible. They looked up at me, and the invaders started to run. I hovered over them until they were far away.

I then flew back to the mountain and landed next to my escort party. Only five of them were still alive. "We lost one of our men," Bussamarai said. "It would have been more if you had not chased the invaders away."

"Your brave warriors will be rewarded in the next life," was all I could think to say in response, before adding, "I shall now return to my own land. Maybe we shall meet again at some future time." With that, I returned to the capsule, set the navigation system on a course for home, and entered the cryostat.

* * *

The magnetic disc came to an automatic stop. "I have now heard your report," the Leader said. "It is unfortunate that, due to your visit, some of the alien beings were killed."

"I too very much regret this," Byamee replied. "The inhabitants of that world were still at the level of settling their differences through violence rather than cooperation."

"What is your conclusion concerning further missions to that blue planet?"

"Venerable Leader, by necessity my time there was short. From what I could see, these are people who still kill animals for food, live in such simple dwellings, and cannot live in peace with their neighbours. But they have learned compassion, and were willing to sacrifice themselves to save me."

"So what is your recommendation about making future visits?"

"I think we should ignore that world for the time being, and concentrate on visiting planets that are likely to be more advanced."

"Very well," the Leader said. "That will be added to your report. Do you have anything to add before we hear from the next explorer?"

Byamee handed over a small package. "This is the picture the artist painted of me. It is the only object I brought back. I would like you to have it."

Aboriginal painting, Property of the author

Mind Games

"Gregory, are going to spend all morning with your head stuck in the puzzle page of the paper?"

Greg looked up at his wife, Anne, who had just entered the lounge. He could tell from her use of his full name, as well as her tone of voice, that she was becoming impatient. Tempting though it was to suggest she went shopping on her own and leave him to enjoy his Saturday morning mind games, forty years of marriage had conditioned him otherwise. "Of course not Annie," he replied," just waiting until you were ready to go out. Where to this time?"

"A new shoe shop has opened in the mall. I'd like to pop in and have a look at what they have and then pick up a few things from the supermarket. We can always stop for a coffee at the café whilst we're there if you like."

Greg sighed inwardly but tried to show a bit of enthusiasm. Should he comment that it was already impossible to open the wardrobe door without being met with an avalanche of shoes? Perhaps not, at least for the moment. "There might even be something there for me, so it's worth a look," he said. "Whilst we're there I'll call at the book shop and see if I can find another volume of brain teasers; I've almost worked my way through the last one I bought there."

"And all the others," Anne commented. "Don't you ever grow tired of sitting there, pencil in hand, pouring over those silly puzzles now that you're retired?"

"No, they're not silly, and many are quite challenging," he replied, making an effort to retain a light tone of voice. "They keep the brain sharp, and you never know when you might have a tricky problem to solve in real life. And you also know I still have that part-time job supporting a local group of students who are studying for their degree by distance learning."

Little more was said during their two-mile drive to the large shopping mall. Anne led the way straight to the shoe shop and was soon engrossed in perusing the extensive selection of footwear intended to lure people into spending money on something they really didn't need. She barely acknowledged Greg telling her he had looked around the men's section but there was nothing to interest him. He would now go along to the book shop and she could meet him there when she was ready.

"Oh hello, Greg. Can't say I'm particularly surprised to see you here again," he heard a voice say behind him.

He turned around to see the smiling face of a fellow member of the men's discussion group that met each month in the church hall. "Hi there, Alan. Good to see you. Yes, I'm just looking to see if there's a new edition of the 'IQ Puzzle Book' available yet, as I've almost completed the previous one."

"I might have known you'd be ahead of the rest of his," his friend replied. "Did you manage to solve them all?"

"Well, most of them eventually, but I'm still struggling with the last one. How about you?"

"Only just over half way through at the moment, and had to cheat with one or two of them," Alan replied. "But I was going to call you later today. We may have a real-life puzzle on our hands if a letter I've just received is to be taken seriously."

"I'm intrigued; do tell me more."

"It was pushed through my letter box last night without a postage stamp. But this is not really the right venue to go into more detail, as there is a confidential aspect to consider. Why don't we meet at the coffee shop a bit later, and we can discuss it at our leisure."

"That might be difficult," said Greg. "Anne will be along soon. She's in the new shoe shop at the moment, no doubt trying on everything they have in stock. Can we make it another time, but as soon as possible? I'm just dying to hear what you have to say."

"Alright, but it can't wait too long," Alan said. "If what I suspect is true, there's some urgency involved here. Just give me a call when you're available to talk." He hurried off without buying anything, leaving Greg to continue his browsing.

He was on his way to pay for what he hoped would be a suitably challenging volume when Anne arrived carrying a bag bearing the logo of the shoe shop. "I see you managed to find something to add to your already impressive collection," he said, making little effort to disguise his opinion of his wife's stockpile of footwear.

"Yes, I've found something ideal to wear at our party next Christmas," she replied, deaf to her husband's little taunt. "Have you finished here? If so let's go for that coffee – I need it after effort of trying on all those shoes."

"I met Alan in the book shop a few minutes ago," Greg said after they had collected their mugs of Americano and taken them to a table near the door. "He says there's something important for the two of us to discuss at the first opportunity. I thought maybe of going round to his house this evening."

"Have you forgotten that we had already agreed to go to the cinema and watch that new romantic comedy the critics are raving about? Do you want to go wandering off and leave me to go on my own?"

"Oh, sorry Anne, it had slipped my mind and of course we can go together," Greg replied, trying to display some enthusiasm. "I shall telephone Alan to see if we can meet tomorrow."

"Right, so long as it's after church, instead of," she muttered. "Whilst you're out I'll see if Muriel wants to come over with her guitar so we can play some tunes together. We need to practise some more before our sing-along at the pensioner's lunch on Monday."

As soon as they were home Greg picked up the phone. "Sorry Alan, but it looks like it'll be tomorrow afternoon before I can meet you. Shall I come over to your house?"

"Sheila will be in then and it would be preferable if we could discuss this out of earshot of anyone else, including our wives," he answered. "Will Anne let you off the leash long enough for you to drive to the golf club after lunch? We can sit on one of the seats outside and enjoy a beer from the bar."

"After acceding to her wishes up to then, I shall insist on it. See you at half past two on Sunday if that's okay." Greg endured the film but could not prevent his mind from repeatedly returning to the mystery that Alan wished to discuss with him. His friend had recently retired from the police force so he would still know many of his ex colleagues; if it were really serious, why did he not just discuss it with them?

Sleep that night eventually came but he would not have remembered anything about what the vicar preached next morning, should anyone have asked him. At last he was free to drive along to the golf club for the meeting. Once settled outside with a pint of ale on the table his curiosity could at last be addressed. "Okay, Alan, what's this all about that's so urgent and important?"

Alan passed a note across the table. "Here, take a look at this. It was pushed through my letter box during the middle of the night on Friday." Greg opened up the single sheet of paper and saw a message that looked as if it had been made using an old typewriter. He softly read it out:

"You put me away for a long stretch and it is now your time to suffer. You thought you were a clever copper so let us see just how clever you are now. If you can not decode this message in time you will not be the only one to go out with a bang."

"If you turn the page over you'll see three cryptic questions. I've been pouring over them every moment I've had but there is one I just can't fathom. Knowing your liking for these puzzles, I'm hoping you'll be able to help."

"Of course I'll try," Greg said. "But why don't you just hand the letter over to your ex colleagues at the station?"

"I thought of that but I doubt they'll take it seriously. Once you've retired you're just another member of the public. I'm sure this letter would be passed on to the detectives but it wouldn't be at the top of their pile. There's some urgency here, so let's look at it first. If we discover anything serious and urgent then I'll certainly go and see them so they can take action."

"Okay," Greg said taking a satisfying drink from his glass. "I can see it starts with one of those familiar sequences of numbers where you have to say what comes next. We have: 3, 5, 9, 17, X. Have you managed to solve this one?"

"I think so, and we can come back to it in a moment. But first have a look at the rest."

"Well, the next one is a sort of poem, but not very grammatically correct. It suggests to me that it's been adapted to include various words even if they seem odd."

"That's a good point, but why don't you read it out," Alan suggested. "It may give us a clue if we can hear how it sounds."

Greg cleared his throat and said softly so others in the area could not overhear:

"Caged I was because of you

Dead I could have been.

Egged on by my so-called mates

A crime I did, then fled the scene.

Add this to my record, then

Gagged and cuffed I was arrested.

Faced with gaol I made a break, and

Ed my sister kept me protected.

Cad that I am, I planned my revenge,

Cede my freedom? No, I shall avenge."

"There's just one more question," Alan said when his friend had finished. "It's another number sequence. It states: 'What is the value of X?' and then there are the numbers 1, 2, 4, 11, X, 22."

"I'm sure we can crack that one, and the first, so it's really down to this weird poem or statement, or whatever it's supposed to be," Greg commented. "There are clues that might reveal who wrote it. It must be someone you had dealings with when you were an active member of the force. Someone was arrested, presumably found guilty of a crime and sent to gaol. But he or she then escaped and was sheltered by a sister called Ed."

Alan nodded. "I've been thinking about that. There are a few possibilities but one case in particular comes to mind. Not long before I retired we arrested a burglar who was also an habitual arsonist and fire raiser. He'd evaded us for quite some time before we eventually nabbed him in the act. We suspected he had a stash of inflammable chemicals somewhere that could be used to make a bomb as well as help start a fire, but never managed to find it."

"This sounds worth following up," Greg said. "Do you remember his name, and did he have a sister called Ed?"

"That's what's been putting me off," Alan replied. "His name was George Griffin, but the underworld used to refer to him as 'Gee-Gee'. And yes, I think he did have a sister although 'Ed' does sound more like a man's name."

"I suppose it could be short for Edwina," Greg suggested. "Did he escape before being consigned to a prison cell as the passage indicated?"

"Not whilst I was there, but I retired soon after he was captured. I'll have to phone one of my old friends at the station and ask him a few questions. He may help me without insisting that we make this an official matter."

"Better be quick about it," Greg commented. "The writer strongly hints that others will suffer, not just you, and that it may be soon. But is there anything else you can remember about this Gee-Gee fellow?"

"Just one thing. When he was in the cells at the station awaiting trial he used to annoy everyone, both the duty officers and other prisoners, with his loud singing. He was always at it, both day and night. The only relief was when exhaustion compelled him to grab a few hours sleep. I'm sure he did it just to make a nuisance of himself."

"Well, it seems as if we can't go much further with the poem until you've spoken with your police friend about this operatic Gee-Gee," said Greg. "But let's have a look at the number questions. The first one is 3, 5, 9, 17, and then we need to say what comes next. You thought you had solved this one, but I can see that the difference between 3 and 5 is 2, and between 5 and 9 is 4. Then between 9 and 17 it is 8 so, if the difference doubles each time, the next number must be 33. Do you agree?"

"Yes, not too difficult, just adding 16. But I wonder what the significance is of 33, now that we have it. Maybe if we can understand what the poem is all about we shall know, but what about the third question. We need to find the value of 'X' in the sequence 1, 2, 4, 7, 11, X, 22. Any ideas?"

"Even easier than the first," Greg replied. "The answer is 16, because this time the difference between the numbers just increases by one so between 1 and 2 it is 1, between 2 and 4 it is 2, between 4 and 7 it is 3, and between 7 and 11 it is 4. So it follows that between 11 and X the difference will be 5, making it 16. To confirm, adding 6 to 16 equals 22, which is what is stated."

"Agreed," Alan said, finishing his beer. "So we have 33 – something – 16."

"Would you mind if I just jot the poem down and take it home so I can ponder over it?" Greg asked.

"Certainly, I'd be grateful if you did this because we might not have much time before whatever is being threatened actually happens," said

Alan. "In the meantime I'll speak with someone at the station about my suspect to see if he did break out of gaol and is still at large. It might help us if this is confirmed so at least we'll then know who we're up against. I'll give you a call tomorrow and report back. Maybe one of us might have made some headway with the poem think by then."

* * *

"Did you have a good rehearsal?" Greg said to Muriel who was just leaving with her guitar as he arrived back home.

"Yes, thank you," she replied. "But sometimes I can't keep up with Anne on the piano – she's a very good player."

"I'm sure you'll do just fine, and all the old folks there will enjoy having a good old sing-along after they've had their lunch."

He went inside and gave his wife a kiss on the cheek. "So you're back, and smelling like a brewery," she said, wafting away his breath. "What was that urgent matter Alan was so keen to share with you?"

"I know you can sometimes be a bit cynical about what I think is important, but this could literally be a matter of life and death," Greg said.

"Sorry, I'm just a bit worried that our performance tomorrow will go well. We're expecting quite a good turnout for the pensioners' lunch this month. Do you want to tell me about it?"

"As I said to Muriel when she was leaving just now, you'll both be fine tomorrow so don't worry about it. I'm dying for a cup of coffee, so let's make one and I'll tell you the story when we're sitting down. You might be able to help, but it has to remain confidential for the moment."

"Right, here it is," Greg said after the coffee had arrived. "You remember that Alan retired from the police force not long ago." Anne nodded. "Well on Friday he received a letter containing cryptic questions. The anonymous writer hints there will be a disaster if the clues are not solved in time. It might be a hoax but we have to take it seriously for moment."

"And did you manage to solve the clues?"

"Only two fairly easy numerical ones. The main item is a weird and rather ungrammatical poem, and we're stuck trying to decipher this."

"Do you want to let me take a look at it?"

Greg unfolded the piece of paper with the message he had copied. "See what you can make of this."

Anne read it through several times. "Yes the wording is certainly odd, but I don't think the writer is just illiterate because the phrasing for some bits is quite good – almost poetic and even with some rhyming."

"Yes, I had the same impression," Greg commented. "There must be a reason why certain words had to be used. Once these had been written down, the message was completed as well as it could be in order to make some sort of sense. If we can pick out the key words then we might have a chance to decode the whole thing."

"Right, let's start with the first line," Anne said. It reads 'Caged I was because of you.' Now why didn't he just write 'I was caged because of you?' It must be that the word 'caged' just had to be written first."

"That's a clever observation," said Greg. "I think you're on to something there. Let's look at the second line to see it the same thing occurs. 'Dead I could have been.' Yes, 'I could have been dead' would have been more grammatical."

Anne read through the message again. "It looks to me as if it's the first word in every line that's the most important. After 'caged' and 'dead' we have 'egged', 'a', 'add', 'gagged', 'faced', 'ed', 'cad' and 'cede'. What comes next in most of the lines seems forced and clumsy, and could have been improved by a simple reordering of some of the words; there must be a reason why this wasn't done."

Greg looked at the paper for the umpteenth time. "You could be right and, now that you mention it, there's something obvious about these words that I should've spotted before."

"And that is?"

"They all contain only the first seven letters of the alphabet!"

"Yes, I'd also missed that. If that is the key, then all we have to do is to work out what is significant about it. Any ideas?"

Once again Greg stared at the poem. "No, nothing strikes me yet. Unless you have the answer, maybe we should just leave it for now to let our minds clear. It must be nearly time for our dinner."

"I might have known your stomach would take over your brain," Anne replied. "But perhaps you're right. Kitchen slave that I am, I'll go and start preparing something and give our brains a rest. It's been said that, once you stop actively trying to solve a problem, your subconscious continues to work on it and the solution then often suddenly springs into the mind."

"Right. Let's hope it does with this puzzle," Greg said as he got up from his chair and switched on the television set.

* * *

Next morning Alan was roused from his sleep by a noise. Turning over to look at the bedside clock he saw it was seven-thirty. He reached out his hand and brought it down on the alarm stop button, but the noise continued. Now fully awake, he realised the sound was piano playing coming from downstairs. Anne was not in bed next to him. What the devil was she doing playing at this early hour?

Pulling on his dressing gown he went downstairs. "Anne, what are you doing? I know you said you were a bit worried about your performance at the pensioners' lunch today, but do you have to wake me up at this time?"

Anne smiled and continued picking out a tune on the keyboard. "I had difficulty sleeping wondering about that cryptic message, but an idea suddenly came to me just like I said it often does when you stop thinking about it."

"Fantastic!" Greg exclaimed, now fully alert. "Do tell me please and put me out of my misery."

"Well, it's obvious there is something that only uses the first seven letters of the alphabet."

"Tell me; tell me!"

"It's the notes on the piano. The scale starts at bottom C and then goes up D, E, F, G, A, B and then top C. Just seven letters can denote any melody, forgetting sharps and flats for the moment."

"Wow, you're a genius," Greg said, giving his wife a hug. "So what you're saying is that there is a hidden tune in this message."

"Not so hidden," Anne continued. "I just picked out the note indicated by just the first letter of each of the ten lines, and played them with different timings and rhythms. One of my efforts makes a recognisable melody. Listen to this tune that begins with the notes C, D, E, A, A, G, F, E, C, and C." Anne then played: do, re, mi, la-la, so, fa, mi, do-do.

"It certainly sounds familiar," Greg said. "I'm sure it comes from one of those musical shows. Let me think a moment. Ah yes, it's from 'My Fair Lady.' Now what's it called?"

"It's the first line of the song 'On the street where you live', written by Lerner and Loewe. We've seen the film more than once."

"Absolutely brilliant," Greg said. "I'm so glad I married a musician! Come and sit down and let's try to put the answers to the three questions together to see if they make any sense."

Once they seated, Greg looked at the notes he'd made. "The solution to the first numerical question is thirty-three, and to the other one it's sixteen. So we have '33, On the street where you live, 16.' Perhaps this refers to the street where Alan lives, as the letter was pushed through his door, not ours."

"I wonder if one of the numbers relates to the address," Anne said. "Number thirty-three can't be a date but it could be the house number. That could leave sixteen as the date when this destruction is planned to take place."

"Blimey, but that's today! If what we've concluded is correct then we need to act quickly. I'd better call Alan right now," Greg said standing up and reaching for the telephone.

"But it's not even eight o'clock, so he might be annoyed to be disturbed at this time," Anne cautioned.

Greg dialled the number. "Sorry to phone you so early, Alan, but this could be very urgent. Thanks to Anne's musical knowledge, we think we have deciphered the message. There was an address hidden in the wording but you had to play it to discover what it was."

"Don't worry about the time," Alan said. "I'm impressed, but what makes it so urgent?"

"We think the event will happen today, and in your street. Do you know who lives at number thirty-three?"

"Not without checking. My house is number one hundred and eighty-seven so it must be right at the other end near where the Community Hall is. I'll quickly drive down there to find out, and then call you back."

"Might as well get dressed and have some breakfast now that we're up," Anne said. "There could be urgent things to do once Alan locates the house."

In what seemed like a long wait, but was only a few minutes, the phone rang. "Alan here. I've driven down my street. The location is not just near the Community Hall, it *is* the Community Hall. The house before it is thirty-one and the one after it is thirty-five. There's no need for a number as everyone just refers to it as 'the hall'. I'd planned to go along there myself today to help setting things up for the pensioners' lunch."

"I'm quite shocked, Alan, because this is also where Anne and her friend will be to lead a sing-song when they've finished eating. Just hold on a moment whilst tell her."

Greg gave Anne the news and saw the horrified look on her face. "We are expecting over fifty people there today, plus all the helpers," she said. "I think we better cancel this immediately."

He quickly relayed this to Alan. "We need to take action quickly if we're to prevent a catastrophe. Are you now going to contact your friends at the station so they can send a squad car down to the hall and make a thorough search of the building?"

"This has all happened so fast, and I'm just trying to think what action to take," Alan said. "It's fortunate you managed to solve the puzzle so quickly. And it does fit with what we know about this singing Gee-Gee, and what he said in the letter about me not being the only one to go out with a bang."

"So then what are you going to do about it? We can't expose Anne and all those other folk to this danger" Greg said, making little effort to hide his anxiety.

"Of course we'll take action," Alan replied in the calm voice of an experienced police officer. "But, if we make it too obvious we're cancelling or searching, it'll warn off the villain and he will only try again at another time and place. We're on to him now, thanks to you two, but we might not be so lucky a second time. These people often hang around so they can see the results of their actions. If we're careful, we might even be able to nab him. Please let's just keep this to ourselves for just a bit longer"

"Okay, sorry Alan, I didn't want to tell you how to do your job. I just don't want Anne and all the others to get hurt."

"What I'll do now is talk to my ex-colleagues and suggest they send just a plainclothes officer, preferably one of the bomb squad," Alan continued. "If you also come along, the three of us can then go to the hall and look as if we're helping to set up the tables and generally get ready for the lunch. However, what we shall really be doing is looking for some device that can explode or start a fire."

"Certainly I'll join you," Greg replied. "But surely we're putting many innocent folk at risk if we just let this go ahead without warning anyone."

"Don't worry; we can take this decision after we've done the search," Alan said. "If there appears to be any risk at all, we shall stop the pensioners arriving and make sure we and all the helpers leave the building."

"Okay, I must accept your experience in these situations. Anne has just told me that the volunteers who are doing the catering will be arriving at ten o'clock, so I'll see you there then."

There was nothing else for them to do but try to calm the nerves and eat some breakfast. "Are you sure we can rely on your friend to do the right thing?" Anne asked after Greg repeated what Alan had said to him.

"I think we'd best going along with him, at least for the moment. He's had many years of experience in these matters. But I don't want you to arrive until you're ready to perform; there'll be enough of us doing all the setting up. If I think there's any danger, I'll phone you before you leave home."

Greg arrived at the Community Hall and joined Alan and the nondescript man he had with him in fetching chairs and folding tables from the storeroom. Without making it too obvious, they made a point of entering every room in the building and carefully looked around for any signs of a hidden device or booby trap that might cause a fire or explosion.

"It's nearly twelve o'clock and the pensioners will be starting to arrive any minute now," Greg said. "So far we've found nothing. If we're correct in thinking this is where your escaped prisoner will strike, we're running out of time. Should we cancel everything right now to avoid a possible disaster?"

"I agree we must make a decision, and quickly," Alan replied. "I'll just ask my police colleague to stand at the door and stop anyone else coming in. For now he can just ask them to wait because everything's not quite ready yet. Then we better go and tell those in the kitchen to stop what they're doing."

Once the officer was in place the two of them went back inside. But before they could say anything Maggie Green, who was leading the catering team, approached them with a look of frustration on her face. "Do either of you know anything about ovens?" she asked.

"Not much, but what's the problem?" Greg said.

"I set the timer to heat up the sausage rolls so they'd be ready for when the pensioners were seated and ready for their food. The timer's working but the oven isn't getting hot. What's so annoying is that a man was in here earlier this week saying he was from the Council and had been asked to carry out a safety check on all the kitchen equipment. If this oven is an example of his handiwork, he's done more harm than good."

Alan's suspicions were immediately aroused. His many years of experience in criminal investigations had attuned him to recognising potential clues that needed following up. There could be more to this than a simple electrical fault. "Did you check this man's identification?" he asked Maggie.

"No, afraid I didn't; I was too busy trying to organise everything for today. But I can't serve cold sausage rolls to all these folk who are expecting a meal properly cooked. I have a reputation to keep up, you know."

Alan persisted. "Is there anything you can tell me about him – appearance, mannerisms, that sort of thing?"

"All I can remember was that he was not a young man, but he had the annoying habit of bursting into song. I had to shut the kitchen door when I was in the hall, just to try and hide the noise," Maggie said. "But can you do anything to help me now?"

"We can try," Alan said, whilst exchanging knowing glances with Greg. "Just give me a moment to have another word with my colleague outside; he needs to know why there's a delay." Seeing the look of exasperation on Maggie's face he quickly added: "We wouldn't want to have an accident with the oven if everyone was inside, would we?"

Maggie went away to continue laying the tables, and Alan quickly returned. "Okay, I've also asked the officer to look out for our operatic Gee-Gee in case he turns up to witness what he anticipates will be a disaster. Let's have a look at this oven, but first of all we must switch the electricity off at the mains. Good, that's stops us getting electrocuted. I see the timer's still working even though there's no power. Interesting. Greg, can you use a kitchen knife to try and unscrew the front of the control panel?"

Once the panel was off, Alan carefully pulled out the wiring connected to the timer. "I can see that the leads to the timer have been disconnected and some new ones fitted in their place. Can you see where the wires go to, Greg?"

"It looks like I'll have to remove the whole side panel from the oven first," he replied. "Good job it's an old, free-standing model otherwise we'd have to pull it out of the recess." With some difficulty Greg managed to unscrew the panel and lift it clear. One glance told them all they needed to know. There, pushed into a space at the back, were two sticks of explosive and a battery. "When these go off the escaped gas will ignite and the whole building will be destroyed," he said.

"Do you think we can safely disconnect the wires from the battery and then reconnect them to the oven?" Alan asked.

"It's a bit risky but we can try," Greg replied. "If we can then we can take out the explosives and set the oven to warm up. Can you see how many minutes are left on the timer?"

"It looks like we've less than a quarter of an hour to make this safe, otherwise we must evacuate the whole area. I'll ask my colleague to come in and see what he can do, as he has more experience with these devices than I have. I'll take his place at the door to stop people entering, so please show him what needs to be done."

The plainclothes officer looked at the booby-trap and then took out a penknife fitted with various attachments. "You never know when these things will come in useful," he said. "Can you see a pair of household rubber gloves I can wear to avoid contaminating the evidence with my fingerprints?" He firstly disconnected the battery and then removed the explosives, depositing both in one of the plastic shopping bags Maggie had used to bring some of the food. "A fairly simple job, not one of the more sophisticated ones I've had to deal with," he commented.

"Well done anyway, it's a great relief. Can we get the oven working now?" said Greg.

The officer nodded and reconnected the wiring to the timer. "I'll just take these dangerous objects away with me now that I'm no longer needed and leave you two guys to carry on. On my way out I'll report the situation to Alan. He might as well let the pensioners come in now."

Greg now did two things, firstly going to find Maggie. "The oven is working properly now," he said without frightening her with the details. "We're going to let the people come in, and you can just explain that the warm food will be delayed a little." The relieved look on her face as she rushed to put in the sausage rolls conveyed more than her muttered words of thanks.

He then telephoned home to speak with Annie. "Can you and Muriel come over right away and start entertaining the pensioners. All is safe now and the lunch is going ahead but has been delayed by about half an hour. I'm sure they'll appreciate some music after having to wait outside for longer than expected. I'll explain everything later."

Relieved that everything was now back on track, Greg went outside to talk with Alan. "The threat is now over but your friend Gee-Gee doesn't know this. I wonder if he'll lurk around to see what happens."

"Just what I was thinking," Alan replied, watching the steady stream of smiling pensioners entering the hall. "Of course he won't dare to enter the building himself."

"Will you recognise him if he comes near?"

"Oh yes, but I don't want him to see me or he'll know we're on to him and stay away. If I give you a brief description, perhaps you can see if anyone resembling this is in the vicinity and doesn't seem to want to move on. I'll just stand back in the doorway so I can't be seen from the road."

It was only five minutes later, after most of the guests had entered, that Greg saw a man who could be the culprit standing a hundred yards away and looking in his direction. "Alan, I think I see him over there underneath the tree," he whispered. "Can you just take a peep without it being noticed?"

"Yes, that's him," Alan confirmed. "I'll phone the station and suggest they send out a squad car right away. Perhaps you'd like to saunter over and invite him in for the lunch. His reaction could be interesting. If you can delay him for a few minutes it'll give the police a chance to get here and arrest him on suspicion of planting the explosives."

Greg gave a friendly wave to the suspect and casually walked across the road. "Good morning my friend. Would you like to come inside and join us for some lunch?" he said, fixing his gaze on the face of the suspect. "The food is being warmed up right now, and we have a few spaces left."

The look Greg observed in the eyes of the man made words superfluous, but he did manage to reply, "'Morning. Thanks for asking, but I was just curious about what was going on in the hall. Now that you've told me, I'll be on my way."

"I'm sure you'll enjoy the sausage rolls; they'll be out of the oven in ten minutes. We're then going to have some entertainment and a song-song."

The man started to move away. Greg wondered if he should try to apprehend him but there was a screech of tyres and the squad car came to a halt right in front of him. The suspect made a dash for it but was soon caught by the officers. Alan came running across the road to help. "How nice to meet you again, Gee-Gee, why don't we all go into the hall and have a nice cup of tea so we can chat about old times and what you've been up to?"

"No, no, we can't go in there now," he replied clearly agitated.

"And why not? Alan asked.

"Well, we don't want to disturb the guests," Gee-Gee replied, realising he was already incriminating himself by resisting. "I don't know why you're holding me; I've done nothing wrong. Let me go so I can be on my way."

"I think you can formally charge him now," Alan said to one of the officers who came in the squad car.

"Very well," the officer confirmed. "George Griffin, I arrest you on suspicion of planting an explosive device in the kitchen of the community hall, with the objective of causing grievous bodily harm to those present, and also for absconding from jail." He then continued with the usual formalities such as the right to remain silent.

"You've no evidence you can pin on me," Gee-Gee responded, an arrogant tone of voice now replacing his earlier fearful one.

"Oh, I think the fingerprints on the device we removed from the oven will be all the evidence we shall need," Alan said. "You can take him away now, officer."

"Well, that was quite an adventure," Greg said when the two of them were alone.

"Indeed, I can't thank you enough for all your help, not to mention that of your wife in solving the puzzle," Alan replied. "I think we can go back into the hall and see if there's a place for us at the table. We've earned it."

As they walked across road Alan said, "I can hear music. Anne and Muriel must have arrived whilst we were busy with our operatic villain."

A smiling Maggie Green greeted them as they came through the door. "Come and sit down, gentlemen, I'm just about to take the sausage rolls out of the oven and serve the rest of the food."

They took their place among the pensioners who were obviously enjoying the pre-lunch entertainment. "We've just time for one more song before the food arrives," Anne said from her seat at the piano. "Let's all join in for a chorus of that number from 'My Fair lady' called 'The Street Where You Live!"

Haunted

The doorbell rang. Giles Needham looked at his watch. Ah, my visitor is exactly on time; very impressive, he thought. He opened the front door and had his first sight of the man he hoped could help him.

"Good morning, Mister Needham," his caller said, doffing his hat and bowing slightly. "I am Cornelius Grimthorpe, exorcist, at your service." He kept his hands behind his back, declining to accept Giles' hand of friendship. "Do forgive me for not wishing to make physical contact, but my powers risk slipping away if I touch someone."

"Of course, I do understand," Giles responded. "Do please come in and make yourself comfortable." He led Grimthorpe down the hall and into the lounge. There was something just a little strange about this person, and it took a few moments for him to deduce what it was. It then came to him: his visitor was decidedly old fashioned in manner and appearance – like a figure from the past.

Firstly there was the hat. Yes, men do still wear them, but a bowler? His dark jacket was double-breasted, and longer than is the current fashion. Underneath it was a chequered waistcoat with many buttons. His attire was complemented by a silver-topped walking cane.

But it was not only Grimthorpe's clothing that seemed outdated. His face sported long sideburns and a drooping, bushy moustache that would have made him a suitable double for Queen Victoria's husband, Prince Albert. There are some very individual fashions around today, but this seemed decidedly anachronistic, Giles concluded.

The two men sat facing each other, at first in silence, each politely waiting for the other to open the conversation. Giles took the initiative. "Mr Grimthorpe, it's good of you come to see me. Can I get you some refreshment – a coffee perhaps?"

"No thank you, Mister Needham," came the reply. "I do not like to eat or drink anything when I am visiting a client. But you wanted to tell me about some strange experiences you have been having in this house."

Giles was still trying to overcome the feeling of unease brought on by the man in front of him. He had invited him to come here in the hope he could eliminate some worries, but the very sight and sound of him were having the opposite effect. Perhaps he was being too hasty in his judgement. After all, reports suggested that Cornelius Grimthorpe was one of the best in his profession.

He rubbed his hand over his balding head, and pushed his spectacles back from the end of his nose. "Yes, we must get down to business. The fact is, my dear wife Muriel sadly passed away in the autumn last year. We'd been married for forty years, and were never apart. I've now been on my own for six months, and strange things are happening that make me think she's come back to haunt me."

"Please accept my sincere condolences on the loss of your loved one," Grimthorpe gently replied. "Can you tell me more about the events you mentioned?"

"Certainly. On most nights when I've retired to bed I start to hear noises coming from the floor boards. But when I get up to investigate, there's nothing to see. Eventually they stop, but then start again in the mornings just as I'm waking up. I call out to Muriel, thinking she must have risen before me, but nobody's there. Perhaps it's just her ghost."

"Very interesting, and I shall investigate this. Is there anything else that concerns you?"

"Well, yes, just a couple of things," Giles said, wondering if he was beginning to sound more neurotic than rational. "When these noises occur, sometimes I can also feel cold air moving around my face, especially in the morning."

Grimthorpe smoothed both sides of his moustache, but otherwise remained impassive. "You hinted there may be more."

"Perhaps it's just my imagination, but I see moving shadows on the wall, and can even sometimes detect a faint smell. Am I being too fanciful?"

"Not at all, Mister Needham. These phenomena are obviously having quite an effect on you and they need to be investigated. You did the right thing in contacting me."

These calm words helped Giles to relax a little. It seemed more like he was talking to a counsellor than an exorcist. "What do you propose to do, now that I've explained my situation?"

"It is really up to you," his visitor replied. "If you believe these happenings are caused by your departed wife trying to contact you, you might want to respond to them. If you let her spirit join with yours, you will be together again."

Giles took out his handkerchief, pretended to blow his nose, and surreptitiously wiped away a tear from the corner of his eye. "That would be wonderful. I do miss her so, and I'd not thought of the situation in the way you've just described it. But what if it's not Muriel?"

"Then it might be a less friendly spirit trying to upset you, knowing that you are experiencing a difficult time struggling to come to terms with your loss."

"I understand. But, now that you've heard my story, can you help me?"

Grimthorpe stood up. "From what you have told me, it appears that all these phenomena are occurring upstairs. If you will permit me, I would like to go there now to investigate."

"Certainly, I'll come with you," Giles said, moving toward the door.

"No, I need to be alone so that I can use all my senses to try and detect what is happening in your bedroom. I promise not to touch or steal anything, and you are welcome to check that everything is in order before I leave."

"I'm sure that won't be necessary; please proceed with your investigation." Giles watched as his visitor went up the stairs, and then went back into the lounge to wait. He heard footsteps going from one room to another, and sometimes it sounded like Grimthorpe was tapping on the floor with his walking cane. After fifteen minutes he returned, and sat down opposite his host.

"I think I can explain what has been going on," he began.

"I'm relieved to hear that," Giles said. "Please tell me what you've found."

"There is a logical explanation for what you have been experiencing. You mentioned noises coming from the floor boards after you have retired to bed, and then again in the morning. I see that you have a hot water boiler in the bathroom, and a timer to switch it on and off."

"That's correct," Giles confirmed. "It's set to heat the radiators during my waking hours. Why do you ask?"

"When radiators start to warm up, the metal expands a little and often emit periodic crackling sounds as they do so," explained Grimthorpe. "A similar thing occurs when they start to cool down again. You have one in your bedroom. Also, I noticed some loose floorboards. If water pipes are running underneath these, the wood might move a little as the heat rises and falls."

"Of course, I can see this now, and I've been meaning to secure those boards," said Giles. "The sound does occur around the time the boiler switches off at night, and on again in the morning. It's been a cold winter, and I've set the temperature quite high. But what about the cold air, the shadows, and the smell?"

"Have you noticed that your bedroom window does not shut properly?" Grimthorpe asked."

"Now that you mention it yes, there's always a small gap at the top. I've been trying to find someone who can and fix it for me."

"Your bedroom faces east, so in the morning you will have the sun streaming through the window. If there is also a strong wind, it will come through the gap. You will feel the draft on your face, and it will bring with it any smell coming from the farmland I saw behind your house. The curtains will move, and you will see patterns of light and shadow on the wall opposite."

Giles lowered his gaze. "I feel quite foolish now that you've explained all this. It's quite clear there is nothing supernatural going on in my bedroom, and I should have realised this myself."

"Please do not reproach yourself, Mister Needham," Grimthorpe quickly responded. "You are still suffering the loss of your beloved wife, and you are in the house alone for the first time in many years. During the transition between waking and sleeping, the mind plays tricks on us and we can experience all sorts of fantasies. Had you noticed that you never have these feelings when you are fully awake?"

"You're quite correct," Giles answered. "I feel to have bothered you for nothing because of my foolishness."

"Not at all," said Grimthorpe. "I am known as 'The Exorcist' but I have yet to come across a case that does not have a rational explanation. People's minds play tricks on them all the time. You may be surprised to learn that I do not actually believe in ghosts."

"Thank you for being so understanding and helpful. But I'm left with a feeling of sadness. Deep down I was hoping that Muriel was really trying to visit me, but now I know it was just my distorted imagination. I really miss her."

"His visitor stood up, preparing himself to depart. "You can still meet her in your dreams. Before you go to sleep, keep telling yourself that you will be reunited with Muriel during the night. If you persist, your wishes will come true."

"I can't thank you enough," Giles said. What is your fee for this service?"

"I shall send you my account. But I must leave you now. Please do not come to the door with me, I shall find my way out."

The Exorcist closed the lounge door behind him, made his way down the hall. He then dematerialised.

Giles wondered why he had not heard the outside door slam shut.

In The Bleak Midwinter

"I don't like it when the clocks go back and the nights draw in," Margaret said in a gloomy tone of voice.

"Oh, you are an old misery," Brian replied jokingly. "Why can't you look on the bright side for once?"

Margaret's response was delayed whilst the waiter brought the tray of coffee and deposited the cups on the table.

"No more sitting on the sunny beach, at least in this country; no more evening barbeques in the back garden," she continued. "What is there to be cheerful about?"

Now retired – she from teaching and he from social work – they had each lost their partners several years ago, but had become acquainted when they both joined a writers group led by local author Holly Keely. Realising they had much in common, their friendship blossomed, and coffee mornings and dinner dates became regular events they looked forward to.

Brian gave a sigh of mock despair. "Think back to when you were a child. First there was Halloween. Didn't you enjoy dressing up and knocking on doors to trick or treat people?"

"Well yes, I did have fun going around with my friends and eating the sweets," Margaret conceded. "But of course I don't do it now, although it's nice to see the little children enjoying themselves," she added, with just a slight hint of cheerfulness.

"And what about bonfire night?" Brian asked. "Maybe it wasn't the same for you, but I carefully saved my pocket money for weeks ahead, then went to the local shop on Saturdays and spent ages choosing fireworks to add to my collection."

"I used to enjoy going to the bonfire organised by families in our street, although I left the fireworks for others to let off. But I didn't like it when the naughty boys threw bangers at me."

"Did you do what I did and take potatoes along with you to put in the embers once the fire had died down?" Brian rolled his eyes with pleasure at the memory. "My, but they tasted lovely even though I always ended up with a mouthful of charcoal."

"I don't remember the potatoes, but it was traditional where I lived in Yorkshire to make parkin' pigs and take them along to eat around the fire," Margaret said. "Parkin' pigs!" Brian exclaimed with a laugh. "What on earth are those?"

Margaret now got into her stride. "You poor creature! I shall just have to make some for you this November the fifth. You mix flour, golden syrup, ginger, sugar, butter and a few other ingredients, roll it out, cut it into shapes, and then bake them in the oven. A lovely warming cake for a cold autumn evening."

Brian took a drink from his coffee cup. "I'll certainly hold you to that!"

"But, once bonfire night is over, life becomes dull again," Margaret said, resuming her mournful tone of voice.

"You're still forgetting the best part of winter – that event which occurs on December the twenty-fifth."

"Oh, Christmas you mean! But that's still a couple of months away, and anyway it's all too commercial these days. Even now in October the shops have already put up their festive displays. Who wants to buy a tree so far ahead of the big day?"

"I do agree we should follow the practice adopted by some other countries, and not allow Christmas goods to be sold before the first of December," Brian said, continuing with his efforts to shake Margaret out of her doldrums. "But you must admit it's nice to go round the big stores and see all colourful baubles and tinsel. It gives you a warm feeling even if it's cold outside."

"Okay, I know I'm being a misery, and of course Christmas is a time to be merry, despite the true meaning often being pushed into the background. It's just that it's so dark for much of the day. I need to see the sunshine if I'm going to feel cheerful."

"You obviously suffer from the winter blues syndrome," suggested Brian. "I believe it helps to have a special lamp on in the house to simulate the sun. I'll put it down on my Christmas list for you."

"Thank you, Brian. You may be right, and I'm sure the lamp will be useful. After Christmas, though, life does become dead and it is difficult to look on the bright side."

"I thought for a moment you were going burst into song, with that Monty Python number 'Always look on the bright side of life'," he said with a laugh. "Or would that have made everyone in the café miserable?"

Margaret managed to squeeze out just a little smile. "With my nightingale voice, I'm sure the other customers would have given me a round of applause."

"When I was a child, playing with all my new toys kept me going for quite a long time after Christmas," Brian quickly continued, pleased to see that his companion might be starting to respond a little to his efforts to lighten her mood. "We couldn't afford many presents, so you tried to make them last a long time."

Margaret nodded. "Yes, I know what you mean, these days children just want more and more, and the electronic gadgets don't always last for long. But once Christmas is over, apart from the New Year's Eve fireworks, there's nothing to brighten up the short days and long nights until the first spring flowers appear."

"You're forgetting the special event in February," Brian said, noting that his companion was slipping back into her negative mood.

"Just remind me," Margaret replied.

"It's Valentines Day!" he exclaimed so loudly that some of the other customers turned to see what was going on. "Don't you remember when we all sent secret messages to those we fancied, hoping they would recognise who sent them and respond accordingly?"

"But those days are a long time ago now," said Margaret. "We're a bit too old now to be flirting like that."

"You certainly are a bit down in the dumps today," Brian commented. "But there's something I have to tell you. I've rented a flat on the island of Madeira for the whole of January, to enjoy some sunshine during the middle of winter."

Margaret looked stunned. "So I shan't even be able to enjoy these outings with you to help me through the difficult time of year." Tears started to fill her eyes.

Brian reached into his pocket and took out a piece of paper. "Here Margaret, I thought you might like see the confirmation from the travel agent. The reservation is for both of us."

She quickly wiped the tears from her eye. "Oh Brian, what a lovely thought. I don't know what to say. But what will people think if we go off together like this?"

Again Brian put his hand in his pocket. "I thought we could make this our honeymoon." He brought out a little box and took out a diamond and sapphire ring. "Margaret, will you marry me?"

The tears once more welled up in her eyes, but this time they were tears of joy. "Yes, yes," she shouted so that everyone in the café could hear, and leaned across to give Brian a kiss. This brought a spontaneous round of applause from those around them.

"So you see," Brian said. "It will not be a bleak midwinter after all!"

The Aliens

"Captain, we are approaching the solar system now," Gork said in his squeaky voice. "Which planet do you wish to explore first?"

Zang raised his cylindrical body from the floor, and shuffled on four of his limbs that served as both hands and feet toward the space vessel's navigation panel. He used his other two to prod some buttons before replying.

"We have seen many gas giants so we can give the outer planets a miss for now. Instead, let us concentrate on the four rocky worlds nearest the central star." Like that of his helmsman, his voice comprised a series of peeps and cheeps, unintelligible to anyone not from his home planet.

"They make a colourful group from this distance," Gork commented. "Shall we start with the outermost one with the rosy hue?"

"Agreed. Our analysis of the atmosphere indicates it is now a dead world. It will be a suitable environment to test our equipment without having to worry about being attacked by aliens, before we move on to the blue planet. We know that one has living creatures of some kind, and they might pose a threat to us."

"Very well, captain, I shall seek a suitable landing site. It will be good to move around on a solid world after all this time on the ship."

And so it was that, after many of our months spent travelling at hypersonic speed from Proxima Centauri B, *Brig One* was brought safely down onto the flat surface of Gusav Crater, located in the mid-latitude region of Mars.

Before any attempt was made to leave the safety of the vessel, Zang sent for the remaining members of his four-man crew. However, the terms 'his' and 'man' did not strictly apply to them. Their species was not made up of distinct males and females – they were all hermaphrodites who cross-fertilised when it was necessary to produce progeny. Like those of the captain and helmsman, individual names followed the convention of having just four letters.

"I have collected some containers of oxygen on my way here," engineer Treb announced, as he emerged through the portal leading to the bridge and settled onto the floor. "Our bodies will be able to tolerate the conditions on this red planet, so we do not need to put on any protective clothing. But from time to time we shall need to supplement the thin atmosphere with small amounts of oxygen."

Last to arrive was biologist Blix, bringing with him a large bundle of leaves freshly picked from the arboretum. "As there is no vegetation on this world, so far as we know, I suggest we eat as much as we can before venturing out." No one dissented, and so these four visitors from a far-away planet rested their two-metre bodies on the deck and, like giant caterpillars, spent the next hour munching their way through the food Blix had brought for them.

Some time later, whilst the weak sun was still high in the heavens, they opened the outer hatch and crawled on their six short limbs down the gang plank. Loading the oxygen containers onto a sledge, along with other equipment they needed, the party headed off in the direction of a dried-up river channel on the crater's southern rim.

* * *

Captain Richard Patton pressed the intercom button to relay his announcement to all crew members of the spaceship *Arthur C. Clarke*. "We shall enter Mars orbit one hour from now. All personnel to the bridge please."

First to arrive was astronomer William Hogan. His specialism was rocky planets. Not only did he know Earth's nearest neighbour like the proverbial back of his hand, but he had also studied those in solar systems orbiting other stars. Whilst visual images of these more distant worlds yielded only minimal information, telescopes operating in other wavelengths had already detected several that had the potential to sustain biological life forms.

"It's been a long trip, Skipper," he said. The other crew members used to tease him about his strong Australian accent, but he was a well-liked member of the ship's company, always making jokes. "Are you ready with your speech when we meet the Martian welcoming committee?"

"Very funny, Cobber, but they wouldn't understand a word of it if I gave the job to you!"

Cosmologist Vladimir Aristov, who was also second in command, arrived on the bridge with Johannes Nguni, the geologist. The two of them had struck up a friendship during the voyage and were often found verbally jousting together. It was not similarities that had drawn them together but rather their differences. Vladimir's socialist heritage had instilled into him the belief that science could explain all the mysteries of life, whereas Johannes came from a religious community in Southern Africa that believed in divine intervention. Such diverse views provided plenty of ammunition for countless debates during their off-duty hours, but it always remained good-humoured.

Last to arrive was Doctor Elizabeth Gibbs. Whilst it was important to have a medical specialist among their number, she also doubled as the ship's astrobiologist. This mission was not expected to encounter any advanced life forms, but tests would be carried out to see if any animal, plant or microbe could have existed on Mars in the distant past. After all, evidence suggested that it did once have running water and a thicker atmosphere.

"We need to make our final decision on where to land," Patton said to the assembled company. "You'll recall that, before we left Earth, we were given several alternatives, but the final choice would be left to us once we had surveyed the planet's surface from our orbit."

He paused to make sure everyone was now focussed on the decision that had to be taken. "Three options were highlighted: Northeast Syrtis, Jezero Crater, and Gusev Crater. Whilst we're performing our first orbit, please consider each of these sites from your particular discipline. Be prepared to state your preference, and the reason for it."

There was little conversation during the next hundred minutes. As the vessel flew over the potential sites, each crew member was far too preoccupied with reviewing data from instrument readings, or using one of the on-board cameras to focus on the landscape below.

"Alright lady and gentlemen," the captain announced. "Let's hear what you have to say. Who wants to start?"

"My preference would be the Gusev crater," Doctor Gibbs replied. "According to evidence obtained from earlier unmanned probes, this site may provide the best chance of revealing any evidence that life once existed on Mars. The opportunity to take some deep soil samples for analysis would be invaluable."

"I agree with Elizabeth," Johannes interjected. "All geological indicators point to this area as being the bed of a dried-up lake. What appears to be a gully that carried water is clearly evident on the southern edge. I too would like to take some samples there."

"Any area named after one of my Russian comrades is good enough for me," Vladimir said, making no effort to hide a broad grin.

The captain turned to the only member who had not yet spoken. "William, do you have any alternative proposal?"

"No Skipper, I've studied earlier photographs sent back of this area and, having just viewed it from orbit, I'm also in favour of landing there, to see just what it's like from the inside of the crater."

"Seems like we're all agreed; Gusev it is," Richard declared. "Everyone take up your positions and prepare for landing. I'll start our descent during the next orbit." After glancing at the control panel, he added: "Estimated touchdown in one hour, fifty-five minutes."

Each crew member now had a defined role. The more relaxed atmosphere abruptly changed to one of undivided attention concerned with what was required during the potentially hazardous landing manoeuvre. The only words to interrupt the silence were spasmodic announcements.

"Course alteration complete. Engage reverse thrusters on my mark," barked the captain.

"Artificial gravity turned off; heat shield in place." Vladimir added.

"Now entering Mars atmosphere;" the vibration felt by the occupants rendered this revelation superfluous.

"Speed now 1,500 kilometres per hour; deploy breaking parachute."

"One thousand metres above surface; ignite landing rockets."

"Rim of crater now passed; height one hundred metres; speed twenty kilometres per hour."

"Stand by for landing. Eight, seven, six, five, four, three, two one. Touch down. The *Arthur C. Clarke* has landed. Welcome to Mars!" The relief of the crew members was evident from the spontaneous cheer that greeted this pronouncement.

Captain Patton allowed the revelry to subside before stating, "I see we're positioned further from the crater rim than intended, so it'll be a longer walk if we want to take samples from there. We should eat something now to sustain us for this excursion."

In addition to the communal supply of water and basic dehydrated foodstuffs, each crew member had a locker stocked with their individual preferences. Much of it still involved reconstituting dried mixtures and heating, or squeezing pastes through tubes, but there were also treats that could be eaten normally such as chocolate, fruit, nuts, and biscuits.

Richard waited until the dining was over and the utensils were cleared away before addressing the crew again. "At least one person must remain on board when exploration parties go out, in case emergency equipment is needed."

"Are you expecting the Martians to come and attack us, Skipper?" William Hogan asked, with a smile.

"Very funny, but you never know what we may find. Seriously though, there's always the possibility of an accident, or delays where we might run out of oxygen. Someone must be available to help."

The captain now turned to face Cosmologist Aristov. "Vladimir, you're my deputy, and therefore best qualified to complete this mission if anything happens to me. I know you're as keen to explore the surface as the rest of us, but I ask that you stay in and mind the shop during this, our first outing. It'll be your turn to go out next time."

"Okay, comrade, understood. I'll remain inside and do the housework whilst the rest of you go out and enjoy yourselves in the fresh air."

"Thanks Vladimir. Our main priority will be to collect samples for biological and geological analysis. The rest of us must now don our space suits and set off. We'll have eight hours of air supply in our backpacks, and we might just need all of it."

Without any further discussion, the four remaining crew members put on their protective gear, checked each other's fastenings to make sure they were secure, and collected their equipment.

"We're ready to enter the air lock now," Richard said to his number two. "Open the outer hatch when the pressure equals that outside." A few minutes later the landing party exited the vessel, stepped onto Martian soil, and set off in a southerly direction.

* * *

"It looks like we have arrived at the dried river channel," Captain Zang observed. "Blix, I suggest you take your samples now. Then, after we have rested a while, we shall have plenty of time to have a look at the more central region before nightfall."

The biologist took out some probes from the sledge and, with Treb's help, inserted them into the soil as far as they would go. After depositing the contents into small boxes, he commented, "I think these will be sufficient for now. I look forward to analysing them when we return to the ship; hopefully it will resolve the issue of whether or not there ever was any form of life here."

Blix returned the tools and boxes to the sledge and, after a short break for sniffing some of the oxygen, the party left the crater rim and headed northwards across the central plain. "What are your plans now, captain?" Gork asked, as they pattered along on their stubby limbs, trying to prevent their sausage-like bodies from sinking into the Martian dust.

"We made good time getting to the rim, so we now have the chance go part of the way toward the middle of the crater. We can then take more samples before doubling back to our vessel before nightfall."

Engineer Treb had not said much up to this time. It was his turn to pull the sledge, and he was content to let others do the talking. But now he muttered – if that term can be used for a species whose language comprised squeaks and cheeps – "If we visit this planet again, it would be a good idea to bring some transport. Not only would it carry the gear, but we could then explore much further than we can on this trip."

Zang agreed. "I shall note this in my report when we return to our home world."

The group continued in silence for a while before Helmsman Gork commented, "This place has a stark beauty all of its own. It is as if we are viewing the landscape through a red-tinted visor. Everything is so still; how fascinating it would be if something moving suddenly appeared."

"Ah, you are just being a romantic," Blix responded. But had they been able to twist their almost non-existent necks and look behind them, they would have seen that Gork's wish was about to be granted.

"Time for another break to refresh ourselves with oxygen," the captain announced.

As they took it in turns to breath in some of the gas from the containers being carried on the sledge, Treb glanced backward at the trail they had left in the Martian dust. "Captain," he blurted out, "Look over there in the distance. There is something moving, I am sure."

Zang followed the direction of his engineer's gaze. "Calm down, my friend; we know there are no living creatures here. I can see what you are referring to, and it must be some natural phenomenon related to the environment."

They continued to watch the anomaly for a few more minutes as it grew closer. "Now that we can see it more clearly," said Blix, "I agree that it does not appear to be a biological form. In fact, there is another one now, a little further away."

"We must stay here and watch until they have gone past, and be ready to take any necessary action to protect ourselves," the captain instructed.

"Is it my imagination, or is there a wind starting to blow?" Gork asked.

"I can feel it too," agreed Treb. "And the objects now look like small whirlpools of dust. Obviously they must have been created by this wind. If it does not become any stronger, I doubt we shall have much to worry about."

They watched with fascination as the two dust devils approached, and then passed harmlessly by two hundred metres to the north of them. As the spirals disappeared into the distance, Gork said, "This wind is now starting to blow the dust everywhere. We are a long way from the safety of *Brig One*, and I hope we do not lose our way. Should we change direction and head back toward our ship?"

Zang faced his other two crewmen. "Do you agree with your colleague, or would you prefer to continue to the central region?"

It was Blix who answered first. "Captain, I can take my next sample another day. We are not familiar with the weather conditions on this red planet. It would be safer if we were aboard our vessel."

Treb had no objections. "Right then, we shall return to the safety of the ship. My navigation reading indicates we head north-west; we should be back at base in two hours."

They continued on their way after refreshing themselves again with a few breaths of oxygen. The wind grew ever stronger, and the small band of explorers soon found themselves in the midst of a full-blown dust storm. "Captain, my eyes are blinded by the dust, and my legs are sinking into the sand. I cannot continue to pull the sledge," shouted Gork.

Zang called a halt. "Stay calm my friend. We are explorers, and must expect to be faced with new challenges. Two of us must pull the sledge, and take it in turns. Yes, it is becoming difficult to see anything in this storm, but I am sure the navigation instrument will guide us back to our ship." Only partly reassured by their captain's encouraging words, the party continued on its way.

* * *

After an hour of steady walking, made easier by gravity less than half that of Earth, Captain Patton ordered a short break whilst he consulted his navigation device. "I estimate we've travelled four kilometres, and the crater rim is another twelve from here. Completing the round trip would leave us with no oxygen reserves, and we'll be in serious trouble if we experience any delays."

Doctor Gibbs nodded. "There'll also be a sharp temperature drop when night falls, and we'd be in danger of hypothermia if we were still outside, even wearing our suits. To be on the safe side, I recommend we aim to be back on board with at least one hour to spare."

"It'll be a big disappointment if we can't take samples at the rim, where there's most likely to be evidence that reveals whether or not there was once life on Mars." This was geologist Johannes Nguni speaking. "We've come a long way for this opportunity; I would be prepared to take the risk, even if I went alone."

"I admire your courage, Johannes," Richard replied. "But you're aware of the safety rules we're obliged to follow – and for good reason. Nobody must venture out on the surface unless accompanied by at least one other person."

"Skipper, what if we split into two parties?" William suggested.

"Carry on, I'm listening."

The Australian warmed to his task. "We can stay together until we're half way to the rim. Then Johannes and I will continue onwards, whilst you and Elizabeth return to the ship. You can then collect some spare oxygen cylinders and bring them out to us at the half-way point."

"It's a clever plan," the captain conceded. "But there's still a risk that you may become delayed or lost, and not make it back in time."

"We Aussies are used to taking risks," William said with a laugh. "Otherwise we could not have succeeded in making our country the best in the world! Anyway, we shan't get lost. Even if the homing mechanism on our navigation device fails, we can just follow the trail back that we are now leaving in the dust."

"Okay, we'll remain together until the halfway point, then stop and make a decision before we go any further, Richard conceded." An hour later they stopped again. "I estimate that we're now at the mid point, and it's time to decide what to do. It must be unanimous. Johannes, are you still keen to press on to the rim?"

"Yes, captain. Even if we don't do this now, the distance will still be the same if we want to take samples from there in the future."

"William, have you changed your mind?"

"No Skipper. If Johannes still wants to do it, then I'm happy to go along with him and hold his hand."

"Elizabeth; your turn."

"Richard, I would be reluctant to veto this idea, but I do think there are risks. There's a lot we don't know about this planet, and we may yet be surprised. However, the samples taken from the rim, especially near what we think was once a water channel, will be invaluable in our search for evidence that life once existed on Mars. On balance, my answer is yes."

"Thank you. I guess it's up to me then. As leader of this expedition, the safety of all of us is paramount, and I share our good doctor's initial reservations. But, I'll sanction the plan, provided all precautions are taken."

There was little more to say, except not to take any risks, and to make radio contact be made each hour. "We shall see you both here, four hours from now, and good luck," were Richard's parting comments to his geologist and astronomer as they off in the direction of the southern rim.

He then called Vladimir to ask him to have the spare oxygen cylinders ready in the air lock.

"We don't want to waste time by having to enter and exit the ship again just to collect them," he said to Elizabeth as they headed back to the ship.

"It feels like we've been let out of school early," William remarked, as he and Johannes made their way southwards with renewed energy.

"Yebo, I agree." The geologist could not resist slipping in the occasional Zulu word, as a reminder to others of his ancestry. "It's we who will take the vital samples that resolve the question of whether or not there ever was life on the red planet. I can just see the motorcade now, with you and I waving to the cheering crowds as we're given our rightful hero's welcome."

They continued on in silence for a while, buoyed along by their shared sense of humour, plus the anticipation of being the first to see the crater rim. Something then caught William's eye. "Hey Johannes, do you see something moving over there, in the distance?"

His colleague peered toward the horizon. "You're right, there *is* something moving, and it's coming toward us, or should I say *they* are coming toward us." All levity immediately ceased, and the training that all astronauts receive for dealing with the unexpected clicked into place. "I suggest we just keep still and wait until we can identify what they are."

It only took another minute before William once again saw the funny side of their earlier concern. "We've seen dust devils several times on images beamed back from the unmanned probes, and now a couple of these little darlings have come to welcome us." They watched with fascination as the dusty whirlpools passed harmlessly by.

"I wonder if the captain and Elizabeth will also see our two friends," Johannes commented as they resumed their journey. "Perhaps I should radio a message back to them now."

There was once again silence as they walked on, before the jovial Australian said, "I know it's dangerous, but I've been thinking."

His companion had quickly learned that the best response to a jokey statement was an equally jokey reply. "I'll stay well away whilst you get it out of your system and tell me."

"If there are dust devils, then there must be a wind to power them. We can't feel this with our space suits, but is the atmosphere starting to become a bit hazy to you?"

"Now that you mention it, I agree. We've seen dust storms in the images sent back to us. If one is brewing up now, we may have to review our plans."

"It'll be a shame if we have to abandon our attempt to reach the crater wall," William said. "I suggest we keep going for the present, but keep an eye on the weather." Still unable to resist the opportunity to make a joke, he added, "We have an obsession of talking about the weather back on Earth, but I never imagined that we'd end up doing the same thing on Mars!"

They continued on but, if they thought they only had one thing to worry about, they were in for a surprise. Johannes stopped suddenly. "Have we been going round in circles?" he asked.

"I don't think so. Why do you ask?"

"Just look at those trails in the sand. If we didn't make them, then what – or even who – did? It looks like something has been dragged along, and there are other marks that I can't identify."

William bent down and took a close look. "You're quite right. Could these have been made by the dust devils, or maybe even rocks that have been blown along by the wind?"

"Unlikely. I've also been wondering if one of the rovers sent from Earth could have passed this way. Probes did visit this area, which is why we chose to have a look at it ourselves, but these are not rover tracks."

"Then we've no explanation at this time. We're part of the first manned mission to Mars, and there's no other inhabited planet in our solar system that could have landed here. There may be a simple explanation, but now we have to take a responsible approach and be aware of possible danger."

"I agree," said Johannes. "And whilst we've been deliberating this, the wind has definitely become much stronger. Visibility is now significantly reduced. It's time to review our plans."

"Afraid you're right, mate. Let me just contact the Skipper and see what he has to say." After several abortive attempts to do so, William said, "There's a lot of static interfering with the transmission, and I can't get any response. We'll just have to make our own decision. What do you think, Johannes?"

"It would be suicide to continue in these conditions, plus there's the as yet unsolved mystery of these tracks. I recommend we turn back now and head for the safety of the ship."

"Unfortunately I have to agree with you, my friend. We'll just have to hope there'll be another chance to collect the samples from the rim but, just in case, let's take a contingency one now."

After taking the samples, they turned around and started to follow the footprints they'd left during their outward journey – footprints that were already starting to become obliterated by the increasing power of the storm.

* * *

Conditions were difficult for Captain Zang and his party. Despite his encouragement, their short limbs struggled to make progress in the soft sand whipped up by the wind. Despite the increasing number of stops to refresh themselves with oxygen, they were close to exhaustion.

Blix stopped. "I do not think I can continue much further," he said. "How much longer will it be before we reach our vessel?"

"It is hard to estimate because our progress has been slow," Zang replied. "Also, I am not certain my navigation instrument is giving accurate readings in this storm. Let us take a short rest before continuing."

They pressed ahead as best they could, but with rapidly declining energy. Their silence was suddenly broken by an excited shout from engineer Treb. "Captain, I can see a large shape looming up through the dust, just over there. It may be *Brig One*." He pointed with one of his limbs to a dark shape just visible a hundred metres to the left.

"Yes, there is something there alright. Let us take a closer look. With spirits uplifted, the four explorers approached the object. But then disappointment; it was not their vessel.

"It does appear to be a space ship, but not one of our designs; obviously it was made by an alien species," observed Zang. "No sign of life that we can see. Perhaps it was just an unmanned cargo transporter, or one that was abandoned for some reason. Let us see if it can offer us any shelter from the storm."

They walked around the *Arthur C. Clark* and soon came to the airlock, left open ready for Richard and Elizabeth to collect the oxygen cylinders. Desperate to escape the blinding dust storm and find a place to rest, the party needed little encouragement to squeeze into the interior.

"It is a relief to be out of the storm and onto a solid surface," said Blix. "But the wind is blowing dust in through the doorway. Is there a way of closing it?"

Treb looked around the tiny space with his engineer's eye. "This must be where the cargo was stored, captain. There are some containers of what could be gas in the corner. Ah, this lever here might seal the door. Shall I use it?"

"Proceed," said Zang. "You can always reverse it if necessary." Treb had to ask Gork to help and, with four hands pulling down on the lever, the airlock door closed. The little space immediately started to fill with oxygen-rich air.

Sitting in the control room, trying to make an effort to stay awake with little to occupy him, cosmologist Vladimir Aristov suddenly saw a red light blink on one of the instrument panels. "That's strange," he muttered. "Richard and Elizabeth must have entered the airlock without warning me. I thought they said they'd just collect the cylinders and then leave without coming inside."

The inner hatch opened automatically once the air pressure equalled that of the control room. Vladimir looked into the airlock, and his gaze was met with the sight of four pairs of small eyes staring back at him. "What the hell . . . !" he blurted out, rapidly taking as many steps backward as space permitted. "I'm being invaded by giant caterpillars!"

Equally surprised were Zang and his colleagues. "We did not expect to see an alien in here," he said, recovering some of his composure. "I wonder if it is friendly. Let us approach it and show that we pose no threat." They raised themselves up and walked slowly toward the lone crew member, whilst using their squeaking and cheeping voices to assure him of their peaceful intentions.

Vladimir saw the four cylindrical shapes bearing down on him, uttering menacing squeaks and peeps. He could not retreat any further, and the only exit was behind the unwelcome visitors. Looking around for something he could use as a weapon, he grabbed a long screwdriver from the emergency tool rack. Pointing it toward the advancing group he shouted, "Get back, get back, I don't want to have to use this."

"Perhaps this is how they welcome visitors," Zang said. They reached the crewman, reared up until they were standing on just two limbs, and offered their other four as a symbol of greeting. Vladimir saw what seemed to be a forest of short hands reaching out to touch him. Believing he had no alternative but to fight, he thrust the screw driver at the nearest invader. It penetrated deep into Treb's upper body, causing a stream of pink fluid to pour out of the wound.

Seeing their colleague fall to the ground, writhing in pain, prompted the remaining three to instinctively respond by falling upon Vladimir. They had no weapons, but instead used the aggressive behaviour that had evolved over the centuries. Biting and sucking with their mouthparts, they slowly but remorselessly drained the unfortunate Russian cosmologist of every drop of his blood.

"It is a pity we had to do that to the first member of an alien species we have met, said Zang.

"If this one is from the blue planet, and his hostile behaviour is typical of the inhabitants there, it would be too risky to visit that world on this mission."

"I agree with you, captain," Blix said, dropping on to all six limbs and examining Treb, who was lying motionless on the floor. "Our engineer is no longer with us; his essence has now crossed the divide and entered the universe of the departed."

Gork had spoken very little during the last hour, having suffered the most from the effects of the storm. "What shall we do with Treb's body?" he asked. "It is too large to fit on the sledge, and too heavy for us to carry."

"The essence has already left it, so we can leave it here," Zang replied. "I am sure other aliens came in this vessel, and they could return at any moment. They have one of their own lifeless forms to deal with, and may think there was a battle to the death between just the two individuals."

"From what you say about the other aliens returning, it would be wise if we left this vessel as soon as possible," Blix said.

"Agreed. This oxygen-rich atmosphere has refreshed us, but it will become toxic if we remain any longer. If we are able to work the controls of the entrance chamber, we should leave now."

Five minutes later the three of them were outside again. Captain Zang consulted his navigation device. "I have computed a revised heading to *Brig One*, and am confident we shall arrive there before nightfall." They set off, dragging their sledge along with them.

* * *

"I wonder why Johannes or William have not called in yet," Richard said when he and Elizabeth were over halfway back to the *Arthur C. Clark*. "I'll just have to contact them myself." After several attempts he commented, "Nothing but static. Either they've switched off, or something is interfering with the transmission. Let's see if Vladimir answers. No, I'm not getting anything there either."

"Do you notice the dust blowing up?" Elizabeth asked. "If this is the start of a major storm, we've seen from our unmanned probes just how disruptive they can be. Perhaps this is what's interfering with our radio transmissions."

"Now that you mention it, you're right. We've a potentially hazardous situation on our hands. I just hope our two friends will recognise this for themselves, and decide to abort their attempt to reach the rim. They should head back to the ship as soon as possible."

"Yes, and that goes for us as well," the doctor added. "We should be there in less than an hour if we have no mishaps, and can then use the more powerful radio to try and reach them. For now, I suggest we just conserve our energy and get to the vessel before the storm worsens."

Conditions were deteriorating more quickly than they had anticipated, as their ship came into view. "Did we really make all these marks in the sand as we departed earlier today?" Richard asked, looking down at the many indentations near the airlock entrance. "It looks like objects have been dragged along, and there seem to be trails going in different directions."

"Are you sure it's not just the wind blowing the sand around?" Elizabeth replied. "Anyway, I see the oxygen cylinders are in the airlock. Shall we just replace our own, and then take another two to the halfway point as quickly as we can?"

"I think we'll just check on Vladimir first, as I couldn't reach him on the radio." They entered the airlock, closed the outer door, and waited for the pumps to start automatically. The inner hatch opened. The two astronauts removed their helmets and stepped into the control room. They could not have anticipated the sight that met their eyes.

Elizabeth immediately rushed over to the dehydrated body of their Russian crew member. "Captain, there are bite marks all over him, and he's been sucked dry. Poor man, he must have suffered terribly, but there's nothing we can do for him now."

"Here's the culprit," Richard said, pointing to the sausage-shaped creature on the floor, still oozing its sticky life-blood. "We certainly didn't expect to encounter life forms like this on our mission. As far I can tell, it's also dead. It looks like Vladimir managed to stab it with this screwdriver."

Elizabeth tried to maintain some of the composure expected of a trained medical practitioner. "It's tragic that our first meeting with obviously intelligent life from elsewhere in the universe has resulted in the death of not only one of us, but of the creature as well. An opportunity has been lost." She paused to let her emotional state calm a little. "What are we going to do with the bodies?"

"We can't take either of them back with us to Earth. Vladimir will have to be buried on Mars; I think he would have wished this, and he'll be a hero in his homeland when we say he died bravely fighting off an evil creature that tried to take over the ship."

"Yes, you're correct, Richard. We can't take him home with us. But this creature that attacked him will be of great interest to medical science; it's the first example ever seen of life from another world. I wonder where it's from."

"Not from Mars, I'm sure," Richard said. "This means there must be another vessel somewhere in the vicinity. Judging from all that disturbed sand near the airlock, there could be several others like it nearby. Perhaps they'll want to come back for the body of their colleague."

"What a thought," Elizabeth said with a shiver. "In that case, I'll carry out what analysis I can, take tissue samples, and many photographs. We can then leave the corpse outside in case its friends return. To prevent the danger of infection, we'll then have to spray the cabin, and seal it for an hour."

"Right, start immediately. But we still have the small matter of taking the oxygen to Johannes and William. If they did make it to the crater rim, there's a serious risk they'll run out of air before they reach the ship."

The doctor hesitated before starting her investigation. "But won't that be too risky? If we both leave the ship, our caterpillar friends might return. Regulations don't allow one person to go out onto the surface alone. Even if we broke the rules, justified because of the emergency, it'd be dangerous both for the one who goes and the one who stays."

"You're quite right, Elizabeth, although we might yet end up having to take some risks. But first let me try to contact them on the more powerful ship's radio."

"Hello, hello," William said when the radio receiver in his helmet indicated a caller was trying to reach him.

"Is that you, William?" the familiar voice of his captain asked against a strong background of atmospheric cackling.

"Skipper, am I glad to hear from you! I tried to reach you earlier but there was no response, only a lot of static. It's nearly as bad now, but I can just make out your voice. Please speak slowly."

"Elizabeth and I are now back on board, and I'm using the more powerful ship's radio," Richard said. "You must have tried to call when we were still on the surface, with only the suit intercom. Please report your status."

"Because the storm is so severe, Johannes and I agreed that we had no alternative but to abort our journey to the rim. We're now attempting to follow our tracks back to the *Arthur C. Clark*, but the wind has almost obliterated them. Can you activate the homing beacon so we can try to pick up the signal to guide us?"

"Affirmative, and I hope it helps you," Richard said. "I have to warn you that it's not certain we can bring the spare oxygen to the halfway point. There's been an emergency on board, and Vladimir is dead."

William, and Johannes who was also following the conversation, were stunned into silence for a few moments, and it was the latter who spoke first. "Captain, the reception is very bad, and I'm not sure we heard correctly. Please repeat."

"Vladimir is dead. I can't explain the circumstances now, but be warned there might be living creatures other than ourselves in the area. Elizabeth and I have things we must do immediately. Even without this, the dust storm is so bad that it would be risky if everyone was out on the surface together. If you don't get the spare oxygen, do you think you can make it back to the ship?"

"Skipper, it's me again," said William. "I'm devastated to hear about Vladimir. But, to answer your question, we saved about an hour when we aborted the attempt to reach the rim. However, progress is now slow and difficult, and wee are probably using greater amounts of oxygen than normal. If we can keep going, we should be able to manage but there'll be little left in the tanks."

"Very well," Richard responded. "Do your best and follow the homing beacon. Now that we've established radio contact, call in if you run into difficulty. Good luck. Over and out."

Without any more words being spoken, William and Johannes checked their heading with the beacon, then continued their attempt to battle the storm and return to the ship.

Richard and Elizabeth also said little as they proceeded to carry out the unenviable work that had to be done. The captain collected a body bag from the ship's store – perhaps the least likely item he expected to be using on this mission. Carefully sliding Vladimir's lifeless form inside it, he carried it through the airlock and onto the Martian surface a few metres away from the vessel.

Using the largest sampling scoop he could find, he eventually managed to dig a hole big enough for the burial, despite the wind blowing sand back in almost as quickly as he excavated it. Then, reverently interring the remains of his late colleague, he said to himself, 'I wonder if he would have wanted a prayer said over his grave. We sometimes used to discuss religion to while away the time during the long voyage out to Mars, and he made it clear he was an atheist.' Standing in front of the mound, Richard placed Vladimir's suit helmet on top of it, stood to attention, saluted and said aloud, "Rest in peace, comrade."

No sooner had he completed the burial, than Elizabeth emerged from the airlock dragging another body bag containing the remains of their unwelcome visitor. "I've completed all the analysis I can, and sprayed the interior of the vessel with disinfectant. We must now spray each other's suits, and stay outside for an hour to let it do its job."

"Okay, well done. We can just move the body away from the ship, and leave it on the surface in case its friends decide to come back for it."

"Anymore word from William or Johannes?"

"No; I'll just try again now, but it'll only be through the suit's intercom."

After several attempts to obtain a response, Richard commented, "Just as I thought, still no luck. We'll have to wait until we're back on board. The next hour, waiting for the sanitising to be complete, is going to be a long one, especially with the storm raging around our ears."

Elizabeth couldn't help looking nervously around her all the time. "We've already had one visit from the caterpillar brigade, and we don't want another."

"We certainly don't want any more deaths, but it would be interesting to try and make some sort of contact. They are after all explorers like us, and humans have to learn to get on with other forms of intelligent life. One thing we've already learned on this mission is that we're not the only intelligent species in the universe, even if one never existed on Mars."

"But these creatures killed one of us – is that a good example of 'getting on' with others?"

"I wish we knew exactly what happened," Richard replied, trying to calm the still agitated doctor. "Remember that both sides suffered an unfortunate death. Maybe Vladimir struck the first blow. We just don't know."

"You're right, of course, but I'll still be much happier back inside the safety of the *Arthur C. Clark*."

Eventually Elizabeth announced that it was safe to once again enter the ship. "Phew! Am I glad to be back indoors," she said, after removing her space helmet.

"But we might have to go out again," Richard cautioned. "Remember that Johannes and William are still on the surface. They could be lost, short of oxygen, or even fighting the caterpillars. We certainly don't want to lose them as well as Vladimir."

"Of course, I was being selfish. Sorry. We're a team, and must support each other. What do you suggest, Richard?"

"The homing beacon has remained on all the time, so hopefully they've been able to follow it. But first let me try to raise them using the ship's radio, before we make any decision."

"I've tried several times now but no response, I'm afraid, only static," Richard said a few minutes later. "I suggest we try again in fifteen minutes. If we still can't make contact, we'll both have to go out with the spare oxygen cylinders and try to meet up with them."

"It's now time to have one last attempt," the captain said as he moved toward the transmitter.

"Richard!" Elizabeth screeched, still nervous at the thought of having to go outside again. "The airlock pump is working; the caterpillars have come back for the body of their colleague. What can we use to defend ourselves?"

"Calm down. If it is them, we'll just have to try to be friendly. But I'll have this fire extinguisher ready to blast them, just in case."

The seconds ticked by and then the inner door of the airlock opened. "That's a fine welcome you're giving us, Skipper, threatening to blast us with a fire extinguisher after all the trouble we've had getting here!"

Elizabeth rushed forward to great the jovial Australian and his geologist companion. "We were so worried about you both. Why didn't you respond to Richard's attempts to contact you?"

"Sorry, Liz, but with leaving the receiver on all the time to pick up the homing beacon, the batteries ran dry. We had to walk the last kilometre with no signal at all."

"Well done for making it back safely," Richard said. "It's certainly a relief to have you with us again. Get out of your space gear and have some refreshment; we've a lot to talk about."

"We saw what must have been Vladimir's grave as we arrived back at the ship," Johannes said as he started to climb out of his suit. "What happened?"

"It's a long story," Richard replied. "But he was killed by a creature that came into the control room. It looked like there was a fight, and the creature also died."

"What did this attacker look like, and where is its body now?"

Elizabeth chipped in. "It was like a giant caterpillar. I took photographs and tissue samples, and we then left it outside. We thought its colleagues might be coming back into the ship now, but thankfully it was you two."

"It's tragic that we lost Vladimir," said William, his voice starting to choke with emotion. "But we did see some unusual trails in the sand after we left you this morning. It seems now that these could have been made by your caterpillar villains."

"Captain, we can catch up with this later, but I think we have a more urgent matter to discuss," the geologist interjected.

"Go ahead. What's on your mind, Johannes?"

"Remember what we were told during our training. Data from unmanned probes showed that these Martian dust storms can last for a month. If that's the case with this one, we would be confined to the ship for the duration, and the solar panels would be unable to recharge our batteries."

"Yes, this was also on my mind, but you did right to bring this up now," Richard said.

"But there's something even potentially more serious."

"Please explain."

"Marsquakes. I've been keeping an eye on the seismograph, and the readings suggest we're due for a quake at any time. Add this to the dust storm problem, and we've a situation where not only are we unlikely to achieve anything more from this mission, but one that could result in the destruction of this vessel."

"You paint a very bleak picture, Johannes, but that's why we needed your expertise on this trip. The safety of the whole crew is my responsibility, and we've already lost one member. From what you've said, I seem to be left with little option but to immediately curtail this mission and return to Earth. Any comments?"

"Having just been out there for nearly eight hours, I'd be only too pleased to wave this inhospitable place goodbye," commented William.

Elizabeth was still influenced by the thought that their unwelcome visitors might yet pose a threat, but tried not to make this obvious. "Captain, perhaps the main reason for coming here was to see if life forms ever existed on this planet. We have superseded this by now having tissue samples and photographs of an obviously intelligent creature from another world. I'd be content to leave Mars to our caterpillar explorers and head for home."

"Johannes, I think you've already made your views known."

"Yes, Captain. I did collect some samples of rocks and soil on our travels, even though we didn't reach the dried river channel. There'll be plenty of analysis to do."

"Then we're all agreed," Richard said. "Please take up your stations and prepare to launch in four hours."

* * *

Five kilometres to the west of the *Arthur C. Clark*, three exhausted travellers finally arrived at their ship. "Well done, captain, for bringing us safely back; I could not have gone another step pulling this sledge," said Gork.

"Yes, it was difficult," said Zang replied. "But you and Blix managed to keep going. We shall have to think carefully before risking going out again during this storm."

"I shall go and collect some food from the arboretum for us," Blix said after they had entered through the hatch."

"A good idea," the captain commented. "We need to eat and rest, and then we can review what happened today."

Feeling refreshed after munching their way through a large pile of green leaves, it was Zang who initiated the discussion. "The loss of our crew member Treb at the hands of the evil alien is a serious blow. If they come from the blue planet nearer the central star, it would make it a very dangerous place to visit, even if we had weapons."

"I agree," said Blix. "We wanted to explore other worlds and make friends with any other life forms we encountered. But our first experience resulted in the death of our engineer."

"But do remember that we then killed one of them," Gork commented. "Were we a bit hasty? Could we have appeared to be threatening it? It is easy to blame others. Yes, these aliens may actually be aggressive and warlike, but I do not think that should prevent us from trying to make contact with them in the future."

"Those are wise words," said Zang. "I also think this unfortunate experience should not prohibit more attempts to reach out to other species that might inhabit our universe. But that will not be for us on this mission. Our immediate concern now is our own safety in this storm. We cannot explore outside whilst it is raging, so do we just wait until it subsides, or return to our home world?"

"If we stay here, and the aliens also remain, are we going to be faced with more aggression and deaths?" Blix asked.

"It would give us another chance to try and make friends with them, but will that be successful?"

"I have just being checking our power reserves," said Zang, scrutinising the instrument display. "We have enough in reserve to last at least another ten days, so we do not need to leave immediately. Let us see if the storm eases within this time."

An indicator on one of the other displays caught the captain's eye. "Ah, I see our probes show that a vessel has just taken off about five kilometres away from us; it must belong to the aliens, so we are now alone on this red planet. You do not have to worry any more about being attacked, Blix."

There was silence whilst the three remaining crew members considered the implications of this. Was it a relief that a threat had been removed, or was it a missed opportunity to learn about another species?

Captain Zang then put words to his own thoughts, saying quietly, "Farewell, aliens; have a safe journey home. I hope we shall meet you again one day."

The Perfect Au Pair

It was Saturday. The door bell rang. Peter put down the morning newspaper and levered himself out of his easy chair. "I'll get it," he shouted upstairs to his wife Elizabeth.

Standing on the step was an attractive young woman with a suit case by her side. "*Bonjour, Monsieur Saunders,*" she said.

"Do I know you?" Peter asked, trying to think why a French girl already knew his name.

She gave a tinkling laugh. "My name is Janine Prévot. I am your au pair."

"Oh, so sorry Janine, my wife organised this and I'd quite forgotten you'd be arriving this morning. Do please come in," he said, picking up her case.

Once his guest was seated, Peter called up to Elizabeth, "The au pair girl has arrived, dear."

"Bonjour Madam," Janine said, when the lady of the house came into the lounge accompanied by two boisterous youngsters.

"Hello Janine, welcome to our home," his wife said, offering her the hand of friendship. "We're so glad you've finally managed to get here. I was just upstairs getting your room ready."

"Thank you, madam; I'm looking forward to being with you for the next few months." She smiled at the children, now more subdued whilst they made up their minds about this stranger. "These must be the little ones who are going to keep me busy during my stay."

"Yes," Elizabeth replied. "These are our children: Tina is aged six, and attends primary school, and Robbie is four. He just goes to a day nursery two mornings a week so he can meet others of his own age."

"Hello Tina," Janine said, kneeling on the floor and taking the little girl's hand. "I would love to hear what your favourite subject is at school." Tina smiled back but remained silent, still unsure of what to make of the newcomer.

"Hello Robbie, would you like to show me your toys?" The boy laughed, and scampered off to find something to bring to Janine.

"I'm sure they'll take to you very quickly," Elizabeth said. "But let me show you to your room so that you can settle in."

"Well, she seems a nice young lady," Peter said when his wife returned. "You made most of the arrangements, so just remind me of Janine's background."

Elizabeth nodded. "I looked at a website for au pair applicants, and picked out Janine. She's aged twenty, and has completed the first two years of a degree in English and computer science at the University of Bordeaux. In order to have a break, and improve her language skills, she decided to take a year out and apply for an au pair situation."

"And here she is," said Peter. "We certainly need someone like her so we can revert to working the unsociable hours our jobs sometimes demand. My international clients certainly have no respect Greenwich Mean Time. But let's first wait for a few days to see how she copes with the children before we leave her on her own."

* * *

"Tina and Robbie seem to be getting on very well with Janine," Elizabeth commented later in the week. "It's Friday tomorrow and my boss is very keen for me to show a well-off couple around an expensive town house in the evening. There'll be good commission for me if I can land this one."

"And I've been invited to a business dinner with one of our best clients," added Peter. "Are you okay if we leave it to our au pair to look after the children all day, and then put them to bed?"

"I think we can risk it," replied his wife. "We've already seen enough of what she can do, so let's take the opportunity to do our jobs and make some money. I'll just ask her if she's happy with this."

"It's nursery day for Robbie," Elizabeth reminded Janine as she and Peter were leaving for work the next morning. "We'll drop him off there on our way, and take Tina to school. Are you sure you don't mind being left on your own today?"

"Of course not, madam," Janine replied. "I'll pick them both up at the right times and make sure they have enough to eat. You have a good day, and your children will be tucked up in bed by the time you return."

Once the Saunders had left and Janine was alone, she opened her mobile phone and entered a code that allowed her to send ciphered messages. She then typed: 'Marcel, this is agent Q74. Am now alone in the house and have four hours to accomplish my mission.'

The response came quickly. '*Bon*, agent Q74. Keep your line open so I can monitor your progress. Good luck.'

Janine went upstairs and into Peter's study. His desk top computer was on but in sleeping mode. She pressed a key and the screen brightened, displaying 'Enter password.' Inserting a memory stick she'd collected from her room, she entered a code that bypassed the login requirement. The main menu immediately popped up. She texted Marcel, 'Your code worked; I'm in.'

'Good work,' came the reply. 'Can you access his emails?'

Janine found what she was seeking and opened up Peter's recent correspondence. 'Yes, and there are messages from his clients.'

'Forward as many as possible to my encrypted email address.'

'Done,' she texted five minutes later.

'All received. Now go to the sent file and delete your messages to me.'

'OK. Will now leave his computer as it was.'

* * *

Both Tina and Robbie were happy to see Janine when she collected them later in the day. "Would you like to go and play in the park?" she asked after they'd enjoyed the food she'd made for them.

"Ooh, yes please" they answered in unison. "Mummy is usually too busy to take us there when she comes home."

When Elizabeth arrived back at the house she found the children were already in bed and Janine was reading them a story. "Have you had a nice day with your new friend?" she asked them, after giving each a goodnight kiss.

"Oh yes Mummy, Tina answered. "We went to the park, and Nanny made some super food for us."

"They've obviously taken to you, Janine," Elizabeth said as she closed the door to the children's bedroom.

"Thank you, madam; I shall certainly miss them when my time here is done."

"But that won't be for another six months, and maybe you'll come and visit us next year."

Janine smiled. "We'll have to see. But I'm very tired so I'll go to bed myself now, if there's nothing more you wish me to do."

"You don't look happy at all," Elizabeth said to Peter when he arrived home two hours later.

"It's been a disaster. We were supposed to be celebrating a successful year of investments with our client, but earlier today they discovered that a substantial sum had disappeared from their account. They're blaming us for a lapse in security, and even pointing the finger at me as I've done a lot of the work for them."

Elizabeth put her arm around Peter's shoulder. "Oh dear, I'm so sorry. But I'm sure there'll be a rational explanation that'll clear you of any responsibility."

"Let's hope so," he replied. "But I'm shattered now, and shall go to bed."

* * *

"It's time you were up," Elizabeth called out to Janine, knocking on her bedroom door the next morning. There was no response. She opened the door and looked inside. Janine had gone.

* * *

"Welcome back, darling," Marcel said, embracing his girlfriend who had just arrived at Orly Airport, Paris, on the early morning flight from London. "I've already managed to hack into one of the accounts you emailed me, and transferred a million pounds into our Swiss bank account. We're rich!"

Janine laughed. "That's brilliant, and I can't wait to try the same scam again – it was fun."

"Perhaps, but just let this one cool down first. I've already removed Janine Prévot from the list of students seeking overseas jobs, and you are now referred to as Emile DuPont."

"I'll try to get used to that name," she giggled.

"Yes," Marcel said as they reached his car in the parking lot. "You did very well, my love. In fact you were the perfect au pair."

Me Human

Ken shook his umbrella before entering George's house. "We've been lucky with the weather over the last few weeks," he said. "I suppose we were about due for another wet Friday."

"Make yourself at home whilst I just try and send this email," George responded, indicating his open laptop on the sideboard. "I only bought this machine recently, and it's driving me nutty. It seems to have a mind of its own, and is doing its best to stop this message going out."

Ken sat down on a nearby lounge chair. "Is it important? If so, maybe you should just phone whomever it is you're trying to contact."

"It's ironic that I'm trying to complain to the supplier of this machine that it does not always respond properly to my commands, and it's now blocking this outgoing email. Anyone would think it was alive, and was trying to protect itself from being punished."

"Maybe that's just what *is* happening. Be careful that it doesn't suddenly sprout wings and fly away," Ken joked.

"Nope, it still won't send," George said, displaying his frustration. "I'll leave it for now and make us a cup of coffee."

The two men, now well into their retirement years, were childhood buddies who used to live in adjacent streets in Dalestrom Bridge, an industrial town in the north of England. They had lost touch when they each moved to other parts of the country to further their respective careers.

It was George who, after an interval of over half a century, decided to try and trace his friend. When he became a pensioner, he and his wife Elizabeth bought a house close to where he'd lived as a child. His ambition was to write his memoirs, and it was this that ignited the urge to become re-acquainted with Ken so that they could reminisce about their earlier times together. After several sessions on the computer searching the World Wide Web, and following leads that petered out, his perseverance was eventually rewarded.

By a lucky coincidence Ken, and his partner Kathy, now lived in the village of Westbrook, only about a half-hour's bus ride away. They agreed to meet, but would they recognise each other after all these years? George was a year older than his friend, and taller; his once fair hair now white. Bespectacled Ken had grown a beard in his teenage years, and he still had it, but his dark brown hair had almost disappeared, leaving him distinctly thin on top.

Their reunion was joyful, and they agreed to meet at George's house every Friday so they could continue where they'd left off half a century earlier, philosophising about life and generally putting the world to rights. In their younger days they were both interested in science and technology, and often wished they had the money to buy equipment so they could conduct their own experiments. However, George did manage to build a crystal set to listen to radio broadcasts in his bedroom when he was supposed to be asleep.

George brought the coffees into the lounge and sat down opposite his friend.

"What do have in mind for our entertainment today?" Ken asked, gratefully accepting the cup of steaming beverage.

"Well, we've a choice of either going out in the rain, even if it's only as far as the bus stop, or having a lazy day inside and remaining warm and dry. If we did stay here, I could always make you one of my speciality lunches."

"Whilst my taste buds are already drooling at the thought of your attempt at egg and baked beans on toast, we always have the alternative of sending out for a home delivery pizza," Ken replied with only thinly disguised diplomacy.

George made an effort to look pained. "Okay, if you insist; you did say you would pay, didn't you?"

With their choice of dining now settled, Ken said: "The last time we were obliged to stay in because of the weather, you showed a video of the film *I Robot*, which is based on one of Isaac Asimov's science-fiction stories. Are we going to watch something else today?"

"Funny you should mention the film, because ever since then I've been toying with the idea of trying a little thought experiment."

"Sounds intriguing," Ken commented, sipping his coffee. What have you do you have in mind?"

"The movie was based on the idea that one of the robots was able to independently create a new law of robotics. At the time, we debated if an android would ever be able to do something truly independent or creative, and not in any way based on how it had been programmed by humans."

"Yes, I do remember that, and we were pretty much in agreement. At least one of them in the film also showed some emotion, which again is something many people doubt could ever occur with a machine. Are you now thinking that one day androids might develop these human attributes?"

George watched the rain trickling down the window pane for a few seconds before answering." I think that's still debatable. The computer brain can store an infinitesimal number of 'if - then' examples of behaviour, and also learn by experience as well as observation. Our own brains can do the same. How can we then be sure that a new idea is truly creative, rather than just being the product of the learning process?"

"Hmm, you've now made me think more carefully about this," conceded Ken. "Intuitively, I'm still of the opinion there's such a thing as true creativity, which is not the product of logic, learning or reasoning. I also think that only the human brain is capable of it. But is it just wishful thinking on my part?"

"Let's not worry about that for the moment," George said. "After we'd viewed the film, I did some Internet searches for information on the development of androids, and the attempts to make them more human. Now that we're stuck inside the house, perhaps we could have a bit of fun trying to discuss this topic from the point of view of the robot itself. As a parody on the film title, we can call it *Me Human.*"

"Yes, I'm game," said Ken, warming to the idea. "Let me pretend to be a humanised machine, tracing my evolution. I think the development of the computer brain must come first."

George laughed. "Sounds like that'll be fun. Okay, let's see how far we can go. Tell me, Mr Computer, how did you originate?"

"Right," said Ken. "I was born as an abacus, several thousand years ago. Although I couldn't think or do anything for myself, people could manipulate beads on my body to help them perform calculations."

Once again George couldn't suppress a chuckle. "This is beginning to sound like the party game of charades, where people take it in turns to stand up, give some clues about a character they're pretending to be, and then let the others try to guess who it is. But do carry on."

"As an abacus I became more sophisticated over the centuries and was able to perform more difficult computations, although I still relied on human beings to carry out all the operations. But when mechanical gears were devised, I then entered my teenage years."

"Let me guess what this new development was," said George. "Was it the astrolabe that was so useful to early stargazers?"

"You've got it! I'm glad you reminded me of the correct name. In this capacity, astronomers manipulated a series of disks and levers on my body, to enable them to plot the phases of the moon and the movement of the planets. So, as an astrolabe, I had now advanced to the stage where I could make predictions; I could foretell where the heavenly bodies would be on different dates."

"But this still didn't mean you could think for yourself, because your abilities were all part of the program built into the device," commented George. "So we're still a long way from the 'Me Human' idea. What came next?"

"I think most people have heard of Charles Babbage. In the eighteen-hundreds he designed a very complex analytical engine with many rotating shafts. It could be programmed using punched cards, and its output could even be printed. Thus, I had now entered young adulthood and could perform wonderful calculations. I even had something of a memory, but still couldn't think for myself."

"We've probably reached the limit of purely mechanical computational devices," said George. "It's obvious there can never be any human element in machines like these, so we need to enter the age of digital computers."

"I agree," conceded Ken. "Maybe I was just showing off my knowledge. But yes, I must now enter into maturity and embrace full adulthood, so far as computers are concerned."

George interrupted him. "But before you do, let's look at the take-away pizza menu so I can telephone our order. It can take up to an hour before it's delivered. What do you fancy? I sometimes like to have the one with anchovies, as they give a nice salty taste."

"I'll have the one with extra cheese, mushrooms and peppers, on a thin crust bass, please," said Ken, after perusing the options.

Once he'd placed the order, George said: "Continuing with the saga of your evolution as a computer, I think we really ought to mention the work done by Alan Turing and his colleagues at Bletchley Park during World War Two. I visited the site near Milton Keynes some years ago, and it was amazing to see a fully working reconstruction of the 'Colossus' machine he developed. It was just a mass of old- fashioned valves, and rotating reels of paper tape."

"You're quite right," Ken responded. "I shall have to imagine myself as a 'bombe' machine that Turing also helped to create, and having the skill to decrypt the Enigma code the Germans used when transmitting their messages.

This means that, although I'm programmed, I'm able to work through thousands of permutations by myself until I find the solution."

George smiled at the thought of his robotic friend trying to look human with a brain as big as a bombe machine. He continued: "One thing that's not so well known about Turing is that he was also interested in the idea of artificial intelligence. He believed that a computer could be said to 'think' if a person interacting with it couldn't tell it apart from a human being."

"How interesting," said Ken. "I'm assuming he never built such a machine."

"No, he didn't," confirmed George. "But did you know that there's a simple test used today that humans can solve but computers can't? Without waiting for a reply, he continued: "When logging onto a computer programme, have you ever been asked to identify and then type out a word that appears on the screen in a distorted, wavy script?"

"Yes, and I find it irritating to have to do this," Ken said.

"Well, it's difficult or impossible for computers to accomplish, because there are too many possible variations for it to recognise. So, if you can manage it, it shows you are human and not a robot. If you intend to be reborn as an android, then you better make sure you can solve these puzzles!"

"Perhaps one day I will," replied Ken. "But first of all I have to continue my computer development post-Turing, and enter my digital electronic age."

"I look forward to your ideas on that," George said. "However, I see the pizza delivery van is already outside. You kindly said that it was your treat so, if you want to go and collect the grub, I'll fetch the beers from the fridge."

For the next hour, the conversation was confined to the quality of the pizzas and the recent performance of the England international football team. Once the table had been cleared, George returned to their main topic. "We've now entered the age of digital computers, so your development as a humanised robot should be able to advance quickly now."

Ken was happy to continue this little game, and said: "I believe the very first electronic digital computers were developed during World War Two. Although they were very large, and few in number, once the principles had been established progress was rapid. Speed and sophistication, coupled with miniaturisation, enhanced the likelihood that my computerised brain would very soon become a practical reality."

"You're right about the rapid development," agreed George. "I remember the time when the first affordable pocket digital calculators became available.

In the early nineteen-seventies I bought one, and felt really chuffed to be at the cutting edge of technology back then."

Ken continued. "Yes, my progress was rapid. We've only to fast forward a decade or two to the time when computers were small enough to fit inside my robotic head. I could then be constructed to not only look reasonably human, but to also have some ability to behave like one."

"Now," interrupted George, "hardly a day goes by without us seeing previously unimaginable developments in both the physical humanisation of android bodies, and the ability of computerised brains to simulate human behaviour. I think, Ken, that you have now come of age in your evolution as an artificial person."

"No, I'm not quite ready yet to be able to say of myself: 'Me Human.' Even if we assume that, physically, it's difficult to distinguish me from a flesh and blood individual, and that I can see, hear and talk in a natural fashion, there's far more to a living being than just that."

"You're correct of course," confirmed George." The android in the film *I Robot* developed both the ability to feel emotion, and to act creatively. Do you see yourself being eventually able to succeed in these very human attributes?"

Ken thought for a moment. "To mention just one point, I would have to be able to solve the simple test we mentioned earlier – the one with the scrambled letter shapes that computers can't recognise. Yes, I would have the ability to learn and develop my skills, but they would likely still be based on what had been programmed into my computer brain. Would I ever be capable of true creativity? There must be some doubt about this, but who knows what the future will bring."

"I did say when we started this discussion that I'd done a bit of searching on the Internet," said George. "One of the papers I came across speculated that groups of robots might be able to learn from each other purely by observing through their senses, and then trying to repeat what they'd seen."

"Why would that be necessary?" queried Ken. "Surely all programming is done by copying algorithms and other data directly into the computer brain."

"Yes, but this would be an experiment to see how robots could learn from each other, the way humans do," George replied. "Just like with people, there would be small variations in what each machine observed. This could then lead to differences – maybe even improvements – when the observer robot had to repeat the behaviour for itself. This process might ultimately result in the emergence of new and original behaviours, and even the evolution of a unique robot culture or tradition."

"Wow, what a thought!" exclaimed Ken." We're now talking about an independent species. Perhaps this is how creativity can develop, assuming that such observational learning can actually occur with androids. But we still have the small matter of emotion. My development would not be complete unless I could show genuine emotion, such as love, compassion, sadness, and anger."

"I agree," said George. "This is likely to be the big stumbling block. You may look like a human, be able to walk and talk, and perhaps even have some level of creativity as a human. But these attributes alone won't make you equal to a real person. Emotions evolved to maintain social bonds, especially of the family, and to unite us in the face of the enemy or other threats. "

"Indeed, I would still not be able to proclaim 'Me Human.' And I can foresee a potential problem related to this. Could the bond between person and robot become so strong that we would not wish to subject our mechanical friend to danger? If so, that would defeat the whole point of creating machines that are expendable, if and when this becomes necessary in order to preserve human life."

"Yes, I don't think we'd be happy to see a robot that we regard with affection lay down its life to protect ours," George said. "Taking this point even further, there's the small matter of robots being developed as lovers. Could this lead to a decline in the importance of human intimacy – perhaps even a fall in the birth rate?"

Ken stroked his goatee beard whilst he considered this. "Do you know, I'm changing my mind about this whole question. Maybe it would be morally inappropriate to ever create robots to be fully human in every way, especially emotionally. It's put me right off the idea; I shall herewith end my parallel development as an android. No longer will I aim to be able to state: 'Me Human.'"

"Good for you, I prefer you as you are" said George. "And we haven't even touched on the question of robots becoming so sophisticated that they are ready to take over the world, as in the *I Robot* movie."

"I think we can save that for another occasion," Ken replied. "My desire now is to remain human, and one step ahead of the androids. However, time is pressing, and I should be making tracks for home."

Let me make a cuppa to help you on your way." With that, George went into the kitchen and put the kettle on. He was distracted by what sounded to be cackling laughter coming from the lounge. "Is that you laughing at something Ken?" he called out.

"No, not me, but I heard it too. I think the noise is coming from your laptop computer on the sideboard."

They both went over to have a closer look. The lid was open and the camera lens at the top of the screen was pointing toward them. Did it appear to have a red glow about it, or was it just their imagination? The sound that resembled mocking laughter was still coming from the little speakers, but it suddenly stopped as they approached.

"This is now getting beyond a joke," George said, clearly irritated. "I paid a lot of money for it, and am still trying to get my head around all the new features. Instead of me controlling it, it often seems like it's trying to control me."

"Do you think the computer has been listening to us all this time, and is trying to tell us something?" Ken asked, meaning this to be a joke rather than a serious statement. "Is it perhaps trying to have the last laugh at our expense?"

"I don't think I want to know the answer to that question," replied George. With that, he shut the machine down, closed the lid, and went back into the kitchen to finish making the tea.

The Enemy

Funny how you sometimes think of some small event from the past, perhaps even just a few words that were spoken years ago. The boffins tell us that the brain stores every little thing we say and do, but we usually remember only the more important aspects – unless you're getting on a bit like me, in which case you start forgetting everything!

Now where was I? Ah yes. Sometimes something triggers a memory of one of these past episodes, and this has just happened to me. I can remember clearly how I came home from Sunday School, it must have been seventy years ago now, and my mother said, "I see you're back, Oliver. What did you learn today?"

"It was about the Good Samaritan," I replied. "Shall I tell you about it, or do you know the story already?"

"I'd like to hear you tell me all about it," mother said. Well, I gabbled on about how a poor man was beaten up, but was ignored by those who should have helped him. It was the Samaritan, who you would least expect to be friendly, who took pity on him and helped him.

"That's lovely, Oliver. I hope you'll remember this story, and always be ready to help others when they're in difficulty." I felt quite proud to be praised like that.

So what was it that triggered this memory which, until then, had been lurking quietly somewhere in my grey matter? I'd just finished reading the letters that my late father sent back to my mother when he was on active service. Mum had saved them all, but they'd been hidden away in a box of her possessions that we kept after she passed away.

When my dad returned home after the war, she urged him to write a book about his experiences. But he never did. Many who had witnessed the atrocities and suffering that occurred during the conflict were reluctant to talk about them. Having just found the letters, and read them, I can understand his reticence to have to live through all these happenings again in order to commit pen to paper.

However, writing stories is a pursuit I've taken up in my retirement. I was looking for a topic for my next book and, having read my father's war letters, I now have one. Let me share with you just one of the incidents he describes.

He was involved early on in the conflict, and took part in the disastrous Battle of France. It was 1940. The Germans had already invaded the Netherlands and were advancing westwards. The French were confident the defensive fortifications they'd erected along the border would be adequate to keep out the invading enemy. A disastrous mistake! The Maginot Line was to remain the butt of many a joke for years afterwards.

Dad was a lance corporal at the time, and a member of the British Expeditionary Force. He saw action at Amiens, on the River Somme. The letters relate his exploits in a plain, factual way, with little emphasis on the pain and suffering he and his comrades undoubtedly endured. Only now, reading his words after the passage of so many years, and having seen documentaries about the needless sacrifice of so many young men, is it possible to appreciate the emotional hardships inflicted upon them.

Whereas the Germans were well equipped and organised, the British forces were short of equipment and ammunition, at least at that early stage of the war. They were no match for the enemy, who had already taken Abbeville nearer the mouth of the river, and were now advancing on Amiens. Aided by the bombing of the Luftwaffe, the town was taken and the British forces were overcome. Only ten per cent of the troops survived, and were taken capture as prisoners of war.

Several of the infantrymen had received injuries, some of them serious. My father was one of them. He had evaded the main blast of a bomb, but was caught by shrapnel in several parts of his body. One piece had entered the side of his left eye, threatening to slice through the eyeball and embed itself in the socket behind. Urgent medical attention was needed.

The senior officer of the remaining seventy soldiers was a Captain Thomas, and he was doing his best trying to check on the condition of his men after they'd been herded together, pending transportation to a prison camp. When he saw my father, he realised he needed immediate help. There was only a single paramedic among the survivors, and the officer called him over.

After taking a close look at my dad's injuries, he said to the officer, "Sir, I can bandage the lance corporal's wounds, but I don't have any equipment to try and remove the shrapnel from his eye."

"Is there anyone else who can help?" Captain Thomas asked.

"Sorry sir, but I'm the only medic left. But I see there are some French prisoners nearby; perhaps they might have someone with the necessary instruments, and the skill to use them."

The officer called across and used his schoolboy French to ask for the much needed help. The response was a shaking of heads and a raising of arms in that universal gesture of helplessness.

"You'll just have to do the best you can," the captain said. "I must now continue to inspect the others in our group."

The paramedic bandaged my father's body wounds, put some gauze loosely over his injured eye, and administered some pain killers. He then had to leave him and moved on to attend to other injured soldiers.

No one else came to help but, an hour later, one of the German officers made a tour of inspection of his captives. Looking down at my father he said, in passable English, "Ah, and who have we here?"

Trying to remain respectful of a superior officer, even if it were one of the enemy's, Dad replied, "Lance corporal George Lawson, British Expeditionary Force, 5044771, Sir."

"Well, lance corporal, I see you are bandaged, what are your injuries?"

"I have shrapnel in my eye, Sir. The paramedic can't remove it, and I shall probably lose my sight."

Without hesitation, the German officer turned to one of the soldiers accompanying him and said, "Go and find Doctor Schmidt; tell him to come immediately."

A few minutes later the doctor arrived. He took a close look at my father's eye, and then infused it with anaesthetic drops. Taking out a case of surgical instruments, with great care he extracted the piece of shrapnel, placed an antiseptic dressing on the eye and secured it with a bandage. Before Dad had the chance to mumble some words of thanks, both the doctor and the officer disappeared to attend to others.

Reading this episode in my father's letters brought back to me that day when I returned home from Sunday School and told my mother what I'd learned. Dad had experienced something similar to that of the man who was beaten and robbed, left by the roadside, and ignored by those who passed by. His eye was saved not by friendly forces, but through the kindness of a stranger – a stranger who was also an enemy.

Hidden

"I think there might be something down here," Vickie said quietly, stretching her arm as far down the hole as she could. "Can you please bring the light a bit closer."

Brett directed the torch so it illuminated the bottom of the hole, being careful to shield it from anyone looking in their direction. "Are you able to get hold of the object?" he asked, with more than a hint of excitement in his voice.

"Not without shovelling out more sand. I'm going to fall in head first if I try to push my fingers in any further. Of course it might just be another stone but it feels a bit different."

"OK, it looks like we'll just have to enlarge the hole," Brett said as he reached for the folded, short-handled spade that he kept concealed in his backpack. "Move out of the way and I'll try not to damage anything."

He carefully worked the spade around the edge of the hole, lifted out what was in the centre and deposited it on the ground. "Nothing solid in there," he said moving his hand through the small heap of sand. "Are you sure you could feel something?"

"I'm sure. Dig a bit deeper."

Brett repeated the procedure several times whilst Vickie sorted through the spoils. "There it is!" she exclaimed, not fully succeeding in keeping her voice down.

"What have you found?"

She directed the torch onto what was nestling in her hand. "It's a small clay oil lamp, the sort that's been in use for thousands of years. There are burn marks around the spout so it's obviously been used."

"Okay," said Brett. "I'll wrap it carefully and then we should leave here whilst our luck holds. Hopefully we haven't been seen, and we don't want to be caught stealing artefacts. At least we've now something to show for our efforts."

They dumped their backpacks on the rear seat of their four-wheel-drive vehicle and set off on the dusty track away from Petra and back toward their hotel in village of Uum Sayhoun. "Thinking now about what we've just done, I suppose it was a foolish idea to go out in the middle of the night, risking being caught by the guards, just to win a bet," Vickie said, trying to stifle a yawn.

Brett was also starting to feel weary now that his adrenaline rush had subsided. "You're probably right. I know there are those who make a living sneaking out like this when it's dark without paying an entrance fee, in order to dig up souvenirs for tourists who have more money than sense. But it's illegal. Anything found is the property of the Jordanian Department of Antiquities."

Vickie nodded. "Once we've shown the lamp to Ralph and Shirley and made sure they pay for that slap-up dinner tonight, perhaps we should surrender it to the authorities. Hopefully they won't ask us any awkward questions."

* * *

The four friends had known each other since they had moved into the same street when their children were young. They were happy to baby sit for each other and enjoy garden parties at weekends when the British weather permitted. Now that their respective families had left home they sometimes went on holiday together, and this expedition to Petra was their latest venture.

One of Vickie's interests was collecting small objects for what she called her 'Cabinet of Curiosities'. To be eligible for a place on the limited number of shelves, the artefact needed to be something that was unusual, preferably ancient, and might have had an interesting history if it could only speak. Okay, the name she gave her little display was not original, having been the subject of books and a television series, but seeking objects for her own collection was fun and gave her an added purpose to visiting other lands as well as local antique shops.

"Instead of spending money on items for your cabinet, why don't you try to unearth your own?" Brett had said one day as he looked out of the lounge window at the melting snow. "And preferably in a warm country!"

"Do you mean like metal detecting?" Vickie replied.

"Well, that's certainly one possibility, and it's a very popular hobby."

"Yes, but decent equipment doesn't come cheap and, if you find anything of value, you can't just put in your pocket and walk away; there are many regulations that govern what you can keep and what must be surrendered."

"I suppose you're right," Brett conceded. "And there's another important limitation."

"Which is?"

"It only detects metal so items pottery or wood, for example, would be missed."

"So it looks like I must continue to rely on the antique and souvenir shops if my collection is to expand," Vickie said with a sigh.

That was six months ago. Now that the idea had been sown in Vickie's mind, it grew and then blossomed with the proposal that their summer holiday this year would be a trip to Jordan. They would hire an off-road vehicle and drive into the desert areas to see if they could find any buried objects. Ralph and Shirley thought it would be quite an adventure and agreed to go with them and share the cost.

Their first trip was to Wadi Rum, a wide valley featured in the book *Seven Pillars of Wisdom* by T. E. Lawrence, better known as 'Lawrence of Arabia'. Certainly a place with plenty of atmosphere, one of the features of which are figures carved into the rock face. Some of them depict images of what may be gods. They learned that these carvings are called Petroglyphs, and the oldest date back to the fourteenth century. How exciting it would be if they could find carvings – even if just fragments of them – on pieces of rock buried in the sand. Despite several surreptitious digs out of sight of other tourists, they went away empty handed.

"Where to next?" Shirley asked in a tone suggesting the novelty of scratching around without finding anything was starting to lose its novelty.

"Petra is a must-see place to visit in this fascinating country," Vickie replied. "It's just steeped in history that goes back at least two millennia. We've a good chance of finding some artefacts there."

"Okay, Ralph and I certainly want to visit it, although we'll keep to the tourist trail if you're going to dig for treasure again. But let's make a bet. If you find something of interest we'll buy you a slap-up dinner. If you don't find anything, then you buy the dinner. Are you game?"

"Sounds good to me," said Vickie. "What do you think, Brett?"

"I like a challenge, and it gives us an added incentive," he replied.

* * *

It was mid-morning by the time Brett and Vickie managed to rouse themselves and go into the dining room to see if there was anything left to eat. Ralph and Shirley must have had their breakfast earlier and gone for a walk, realising that their friends would be sleeping late after being up for much of the night.

Munching on a piece of toast covered with scrambled egg that had been languishing in a tray on the buffet counter, Vickie said, "I'm glad the others are not here to ask questions. Let's try to avoid them until dinner time, and then surprise them with our find."

Brett gave a big grin. "Great idea, but let's make sure we order the most expensive dishes on the menu before pulling our rabbit out of the magician's hat."

"Actually it'll be my handbag, but the idea will be the same."

"We've been looking for you all day," Ralph said as he and Shirley joined them at the dinner table that evening. "Are you avoiding us or something?"

"Whatever gave you that idea?" Brett responded. "Remember we were outside for much of the night so most of the morning had gone by the time we regained consciousness. This afternoon we needed to get some fresh air. How about you two?"

"We realised you might be sleeping late when you weren't at breakfast, but did think we would see you after lunch. Anyway, never mind, we're all here together now and dying to know if you had any success with your illegal souvenir hunt."

"Let's just order dinner first, and we can chat whilst we're waiting for it to arrive," Vickie said. "I'm told that one really must try the local Mansaf. The menu describes it as comprising rice, lamb and jameed – a sort of hard dried-out fermented goat's milk yogurt."

"And I'll have the Shish Kebabs," said Brett. "I had these at a restaurant in London once, but here is where they originated. It states they're made from minced lamb mixed with parsley and salt, then moulded on to skewers and grilled over hot charcoal. What do you two fancy?"

"Just give us a minute to catch up," Ralph said. "You had the advantage of being here before us."

Eventually all the orders were placed, including starters and drinks. "Now, did you find anything last night, or will you be paying for this dinner?" Shirley asked.

This was the conjurer's moment: "Da Dah!" Vickie sang out, producing the wrapped object from her bag. "What do you think of this?"

Their two friends looked at the lamp, small enough to hold in the palm of the hand, its sooty spout contrasting with the reddish colour of the rest of the clay body. "Well, it looks old and it certainly has been used," Ralph said. "Where did you find this?"

Greg related how they had driven along the back road to Petra and then dug a few holes in the sand before striking lucky with their final attempt. "Do we win the bet and enjoy a free dinner?"

"I guess you do, and well done. But are sure you haven't broken the law by removing this lamp?"

Vickie chipped in: "We did talk about this, and decided we would hand it in to the appropriate authority, hoping they wouldn't ask any awkward questions"

"So we came all this way with the object of finding something for your cabinet of curiosities, and you'll be going home empty-handed," Shirley commented.

"I hope not. There may be something suitable to buy at the visitors centre or an antique shop, where I'd be given the necessary paperwork to show that all is above board."

"Ah, here come the starters," Brett announced. "I'm starving and the grub will taste all the better because we haven't paid for it."

The chatter changed to more general topics, and the food and wine gradually disappeared. All that remained were the after dinner coffees. "Well, I certainly enjoyed that even though it'll cost me a packet," Ralph said. "Just remind me not to make any more hasty bets with you two intrepid explorers."

They didn't notice the head waiter in the doorway pointing in their direction, nor one of the receptionists from the front desk walking toward them. "Excuse me sir, but there are people in reception waiting to see you."

Brett looked up and was surprised to see a smart young woman looking straight at him, the name on the hotel's badge she was wearing indicating she was Maysa Khalil. "Wants to see me, Maysa? Who are they?"

"Yes, sir, just you, and I think you should come right away to meet them." There was a hint of pleading in her voice that suggested it would be preferable not to create a scene and disrupt the other diners.

He excused himself from the table and followed the clerk out of the room. Two men were standing at the desk. "Good evening sir, I am Sergeant Abdel Fayez, and this is Constable Ibrahim Hammad. We are special officers from the Petra police force." They each proffered identity cards bearing an official-looking logo. Because all the writing was in Arabic, Brett was not able to read any of the details.

"But you are not in uniform. How can I be sure you're actually from the police?" Brett asked, noticing a bulge under their clothing that suggested these men were armed.

"We can talk here, or we can take you to the station and discuss this in the charge room," the sergeant replied. "The choice is yours."

"Okay," Brett conceded. "Let's move over to the chairs near the window and you can tell me what this is all about."

"Sir, can you confirm that you are currently renting a four-wheel-drive vehicle with this registration number?" Constable Hammad asked, holding up a piece of paper.

"Yes, this is the one we've been using this week."

"We have a witness that states he saw this car setting out in the dark last night and driving toward the Petra site on the back road, bypassing the rear entrance gate. Were you the driver?"

It was obvious to Brett where this interrogation was leading. "Yes, officer, my wife and I were in the car."

The questions continued. "And what was the purpose of this nocturnal jaunt?"

"We just wanted to experience the dark skies in the desert and look at the stars."

The sergeant now took over. "We have evidence that you were digging in the sand, obviously trying to find buried artefacts as others have done illegally, and that you brought a wrapped object into the hotel on your return. What did you find, and where is it now."

Brett realised he had little alternative but to admit everything and hope for leniency. "You're quite correct, officer, and I'm sorry. We found a small clay lamp, and have just been showing it to our dinner companions."

"Would you please bring it to us, and also your passport."

With as much good grace as he could muster, Brett firstly went to the bedroom to collect his passport, and then to the dining room for the lamp. His wife and friends were anxious to know what was going on, but he had to reply that he would explain everything when he returned.

"Here you are officer," he said, handing over the objects. "Why do you need my passport?"

"To make sure you don't disappear until we've dealt with this matter. You do realise that some of these lamps are worth a lot of money, and that it's illegal to remove them without the necessary permit?"

"Yes, I was feeling guilty about that and my wife and I agreed that we would hand this to the authorities before we left the country. You can ask her if you wish."

"There will be time for that later. Please both of you report to the Petra police station at ten tomorrow morning, when we shall decide on what further action to take," the sergeant said as the two officers stood up. "Once the law has run its course, your passport will be returned to you."

Brett sheepishly returned to his friends at the dinner table. The earlier reverie generated by the fine food helped down by more than one glass of wine, had now been replaced by something more sombre. "Sorry to have dragged you into all this," he said to Ralph and Shirley, after summarising the uncomfortable conversation he'd just had with the two officers. "We'll just have to hope this can be cleared up tomorrow, but I wouldn't want you to miss your return flights because of us."

"Don't worry, we'll stick together," Ralph replied. "I'm sure this'll be resolved quickly even if you have to pay a fine. Let's try to push this into the background for now and have another round of drinks before we turn in."

Despite all the thoughts spinning around in Brett's head, once in bed it didn't take long for the combination of alcohol and lack of sleep the previous night to propel him into slumberland. There was little to be cheerful about over breakfast, which he and Vickie ate alone, their friends presumably enjoying another hour of sleep. Time seemed to move slowly but eventually they prepared to leave for their appointment. They passed Ralph and Shirley on their way out, and tried to take on board their friends exhortations not to worry as they would be there to support them whatever the outcome.

A few minutes later they arrived at the police station and went up to the enquiry desk. "Can I help you?" a cheerful uniformed officer said.

"We are here to see Sergeant Fayez and Constable Hammad," Brett said. "We have an appointment with them for ten o'clock this morning."

"What were those names again?" the officer asked, looking down the list of the station's personnel. Brett repeated the details. "Sorry sir, there's nobody here by either of those names. Hold on a moment whilst I consult my superior."

Two minutes later he returned accompanied by a senior officer. "Good morning sir, madam, I am Inspector Hainzl. My officer here tells me you asked to see a sergeant Fayez and constable Hammad. I've checked the police directory but they are not members of the Jordanian force. Were they in uniform?"

"No, they said they were special officers, and showed me their I.D. documents."

The desk officer took a folded card out of his breast pocket. "Did their documents look anything like this?"

Brett only needed a quick glance. "No. Their papers were all in Arabic and the logo stamped on them was different to yours."

"Inspector Hainzl nodded. "Because we have many tourists, our I.D.s are printed in both English and Arabic so anyone can read them. I think we should all go into an interview room and take full statements from you both."

After he and Vickie had provided their names and other personal details, Brett anticipated the next question: "Please tell us the reason why you were visited by these so-called officers." There was no point in hiding anything, so he admitted to having dug up the lamp without permission but assured the officers he was going to hand it in to the authorities before leaving the country.

"I see," the inspector commented, briefly looking up from the notes he was making. "Did you give them the lamp?"

"Yes, and they also asked for my passport to make sure Vickie and I both reported here this morning. I'm sure they were armed because I could see suspicious-looking bulges under their clothing. It didn't seem advisable to argue with them."

"Probably very wise under the circumstances, sir. Can you give me a description of these two men?"

Brett did his best, but feared it wouldn't be accurate enough to help track them down. He was therefore relieved when the inspector responded: "From what you've told us, we can link these two individuals to other incidents of a similar nature."

"You mean we're not the first to be victims of these impostors?"

"Indeed so. The way they work is to have accomplices in hotels and other tourist venues who keep their eyes and ears open for visitors who are tempted to go digging just like you two did. They then report back to the two ringleaders and receive a share of any profit made when the artefacts are sold."

"So we've been victims of confidence tricksters," Vickie said, unable to hide her anger. "I've been worried sick and it's ruined our holiday. If you've had reports from others who've been tricked, why haven't you caught the villains?"

"Madam," Hainzl said, adopting an authoritative voice, "Remember that you and your husband have broken the law. The penalty for what you've done is a minimum of one year in prison plus a fine."

"Sorry," she replied, now subdued. "But we were going to hand the lamp in."

"Yes, that's what they all say, and we shall consider this in mitigation. And be assured that we've done our best to apprehend these people, and are drawing closer. You and your friends might be able to help us succeed."

"Of course we would be only too willing to help," Brett said. "There is also the matter of my passport."

"If we can catch the villains we shall no doubt retrieve your passport," the inspector said. "And probably also those of other victims who've had to go to their embassies and obtain emergencies papers before they could return home."

"Okay. How can we help to catch these devils?"

"You told us you are with two other friends, but that they didn't accompany you on your illegal dig."

"Yes, that's true."

"Then let's set a trap. Ask them to copy just what you did, spending some time in the desert at night pretending to dig. Let them come back at a similar time with a bundle in their hands, looking pleased as if they'd discovered some treasure."

Brett smiled. "I'm sure they'd have fun doing this, and we can even say we'll buy them dinner if they succeed."

"Excellent," the inspector said. Let this be tonight, and we shall keep watch to see if those two men return. Oh, there's one other thing."

"Which is?"

"We also want to identify the spy who tips off these criminals. All of you see if you can spot anybody at the hotel who appears to be listening to conversations and taking an interest in any artefacts that are being shown or discussed."

Ralph and Shirley were waiting anxiously for their friends to return, and were relieved when they arrived back with even the hint of a smile on their faces. "Right, do tell us what happened," said Ralph. "You were obviously not locked up."

"It would be best if we went a little ride in the car before we say anything," Vickie replied. "There maybe someone at the hotel who's taking an unusual interest in what we have to report."

They drove along one of the desert roads in silence, before stopping at an isolated lay-by. "I'm intrigued by all this cloak and dagger stuff," Shirley said. "Do tell."

Brett related how they'd been hoaxed, even though they'd broken the law. "So are you going to be fined or imprisoned?" Ralph asked when his friend had come to a stop.

"We could be, but the officers at the station thought we might be able to set a trap to catch these criminals. The point is, it would involve you two."

Ignoring the incredulous look on the faces of Ralph and Shirley, Brett outlined the plan.

"What do you both think?" he asked. "Would you be willing to go out at night just like we did, but only pretend to dig for artefacts? I'll add an incentive. If you do, then the special dinner the next evening will be on us."

It didn't take long for the pair to come to a decision. "If you're sure we won't be prosecuted, then it would be fun. Yes, we'll do it tonight," Ralph said.

"Brilliant. Can I just add that, whilst not making it too obvious, drop a few hints about what you intend to do when there are others who might overhear, for example in reception."

Shirley gave a big smile. "It's all quite exciting. But now that everything is agreed why don't we drive on to the main visitor's entrance like good tourists and have a look at the famous Petra Treasury building."

After they'd paid the entrance fee and commenced the three-quarter mile walk down to the main site, Brett said: "I believe this city dates back to about three-hundred years B.C. and was founded by the Nabataeans who roamed the Arabian Desert."

"Amazing what people could build so long ago," Shirley commented. "I'd not heard of Nabataeans before. Do they still exist today?"

"No, at least not as a pure race. They were absorbed into the Roman Empire. Petra was abandoned after about four hundred years, and stayed empty apart from visits by the Crusaders round about the year one thousand."

"I'm impressed, you must have done some reading before we set off on this jaunt," said Shirley. "When was it rediscovered?"

Brett smiled. "Yes, I always do some research on places I'm going to visit. But to answer your question, it was found again by a Swiss explorer called John Burckhardt in the early eighteen-hundreds. But we're just coming to the narrow gorge the locals call The Siq. Once we're through this we'll have a wonderful sight before us."

"Wow! I can almost touch the rocks on both sides at once," Vickie said. "And look how high the cliffs are."

In a few seconds they emerged into the open to be met by the sight of the rose-coloured, temple-like building cut directly into the rock face. Nobody spoke, as no words could do justice to its breath-taking beauty. Eventually they walked past the camels squatting on the ground ready to give tourists a ride, and up to the Treasury entrance. "Does the inside of this building go back a long way?" Ralph asked.

"No, it's quite plain and shallow actually," Brett replied. "And visitors aren't usually allowed in. Once we've feasted our eyes on the impressive façade, let's move on so you and Shirley can form an idea of where you'll come tonight."

They walked on down the slope, noting ruins on the cliffs on both sides, past what was once an amphitheatre, and out onto the plain beyond. "We don't need to go any further," Brett said. "But you can see the road stretching before us, weaving its way past more ruins in various stages of disrepair. When you two come tonight you'll enter through the gate at the far end and then drive about half way along. You can then stop and pretend to do your digging."

Once all questions had been answered, they turned and started to make their way back toward the entrance. "I didn't realise we'd come this far," Shirley said. "And it's all uphill in this oppressive heat."

"I agree," said Brett. "Just take it slowly and we can rest when we reach the entrance building. "Perhaps we should buy a souvenir at the tourist shop and pretend it's what you've dug up. But remember to keep the receipt!"

Back at the hotel it was time for Ralph and Shirley to rest and prepare themselves for their night time adventure.

* * *

Brett and Vickie didn't expect to be joined by their two friends when went down for breakfast the next morning. "I had difficulty trying to get to sleep last night," said Vickie. "I was listening for our four-wheel-drive vehicle leaving the car park."

"And did you?"

"Not sure, but I must have dropped off eventually despite your snoring."

"We'll just have to wait until they turn up later, so let's just be patient and enjoy our breakfast. Assuming our car is back where it should be, we can then go and explore a bit more of this fascinating country and leave our friends to catch up on their rest."

The drive to the southernmost tip of the Dead Sea took longer than expected, but the fun of being able to float on top of the mineral-rich water at this lowest point on Earth dominated their thoughts and feelings. It was only on their way back to the hotel that Vickie raised the matter of their predicament. "Unless the trap that Ralph and Shirley are hoping to set for the criminals is successful, and we convince the real police that we didn't intend to break the law, we could find ourselves in jail in the next few days."

"And my passport is still missing," Brett added. "But let's be positive and continue to enjoy this holiday whilst we can."

Back at the hotel, they resisted the temptation to try and find their two friends, but went straight to their room shower off the mineral deposits left by the Dead Sea. Once they were dressed in their evening clothes, Vickie said, "I suggest we go and sit in the reception area and do some people watching in case we spot anyone who might be involved in this criminal operation."

Indeed there was much activity with people departing, arriving, or just standing there chatting. A cheerful voice alerted them: "Hi you two. Where have you been all day?" It was Ralph, with a big smile on his face, and Shirley was also looking quite pleased with herself.

"Good to see you again," Brett said, briefly relating their trip to the Dead Sea. "We are dying to hear what you've been up to."

"Quite a productive night," Ralph replied, patting a small bundle he was carrying, and making little effort to keep his voice down. "We've got something to show you when we're at our table."

"Sounds exciting," said Vickie, aware of glances in their direction from some of the bystanders. "I can't wait to see what you have in there."

"Just a few more minutes before we can go in for dinner. I assume the meal will be on you tonight, just as you promised."

"If what you have there is what I think it might be, then yes, eat what you want and I'll pay," said Brett.

They went into the dining room and sat down. "Right, let's have a look at what you've found," Vickie asked, knowing full well what was in the parcel. Sure enough it was the modern model of a statue they'd bought earlier at the souvenir shop, but they all responded with 'wow' exclamations as if it was an item from the Crown Jewels.

Moments later they looked up to see a young woman walking toward them. As was the case two evenings ago with Brett and Vickie, it was Maysa Khalil, one of the receptionists. She looked at Ralph and Shirley. "Sir, madam, there are two men in the foyer wishing to speak with you. Would you follow me, please."

They did as requested. When the three of them were out of sight, Brett and Vickie quietly rose to their feet and peeped round door so they could look into the reception area without being seen. They saw their friends meeting the same two bogus policemen as they had done. "Should we go in and confront them?" Vickie whispered. But before Brett could answer, in through the hotel front door came Inspector Hainzel accompanied by four of his uniformed colleagues.

"Let's go in and join the party now and see what the police will do." They reached the others in time to see handcuffs being fitted to Abdel Fayez and Ibrahim Hammad. Although they couldn't understand the local language, it sounded like the inspector was going through the wording of a formal charge.

"Good evening you two," the inspector said to Brett and Vickie. "The plan was successful. Our observers saw your two friends setting off after midnight along the back road to Petra, and then followed them far enough to see that they stopped and started excavating for artefacts.

"It was quite an adventure," Shirley said. "When we came back to the hotel we deliberately talked a lot about what we'd been up to."

"Yes, and the word quickly spread until someone gave these two villains here the tip off," Inspector Hainzl commented. "Miss Khalil," he called over to the reception desk. "Could you please come and join us."

A nervous-looking Maysa walked across to where they were standing. "Yes sir?"

"We've reason to believe you have been acting as an informant for these two criminals, telling them when you suspect one of the guests has been digging for souvenirs."

"Sir, I didn't mean to do anyone harm, but I have a child at home and didn't want anything to happen to him."

"It sounds as if you've been threatened, so don't say anything more now. Just come with us to the police station where we'll formally charge these two characters. You can make a statement there and we can then decide what further action to take."

"Before you go," Brett said to the inspector, "there are the small matters of my passport and the charges against Vickie and me. Our holiday is coming to an end. Are we going to be formally charged for trying to smuggle out an historical artefact? If I'm not in jail, I shall still be unable to leave the country without a passport."

"Don't worry, we've not forgotten, but we knew you wouldn't suddenly disappear before this

matter was concluded. Both of you come to the station tomorrow at mid-day. We'll have concluded our investigations by then." With a final word of thanks to Ralph and Shirley for their help in setting the trap, the police and their prisoners departed, leaving the four friends to return to the dining room and continue their meal at Brett's expense.

"Well, that was the best night's sleep I've had since we booked into this hotel," Brett said when they all met up for breakfast. "I feel quite relaxed even though Vickie and I might be locked up in jail before the day is out."

"Oh I doubt it," Shirley replied. "That inspector seemed a fair person and I'm sure he'll take note of what you say in defence. You've a couple of hours before you need to go to the station, so how about we go a walk around this village? I believe there are some ruins of a Byzantine church if we can find them."

Not realising how far they had walked, Brett and Vickie had to rush back to the hotel and pick up their car for the all-important visit to the police. They arrived on time, if a little breathless, only to find they then had to wait ten minutes before Inspector Hainzl invited them into his office.

"Sorry to keep you waiting, but I have some good news: we have your passport."

"I'm delighted," Brett said. "But where did you find it?"

"Once we'd checked on the two men we arrested yesterday evening, we found they already had a police record but had used different names. They'd previously been found guilty of fraud and the selling of stolen property. We located where they lived and searched the premises. There were at least a dozen passports, including this one belonging to you," the inspector said, sliding the document across the desk.

"Thank you so much; that's a great relief," Brett exclaimed.

"We continued the search and found several boxes of artefacts they were obviously planning to sell. From the description you gave us, we believe this is what you had excavated."

Brett opened the small bundle the inspector had placed in front of him on the desk. "Yes, that's certainly the one Vickie and I found, and then gave to those two criminals."

"That just leaves us with one more matter to deal with," Hainzl said. "And it's a serious one."

"I can guess what's coming," said Vickie, now looking distinctly worried.

The inspector was unsmiling. "Yes, the illegal act you two knowingly committed, intending to rob this kingdom of its treasures."

"That comes across a bit strong," Brett said. "But yes, we did wrong but have already said we were going to surrender the lamp to the authorities before we left Jordan."

"I've discussed your case with my superior and the officer who decides whether or not a case is referred to the law court," Hainzl continued, ignoring this comment. "In the case of Fayez and Hammad this will certainly happen."

"And with Vickie and me?"

"We did take into account your declared intention, and we are also grateful that, with the help of your friends, we've now caught the two criminals who've been preying on tourists." The inspector's face now broadened into a big smile. "In view of this we have given you the benefit of the doubt and you will not be charged."

Vickie wiped a small tear from the corner of her eye. "Oh thank you, thank you. It has been a worry. I want to give you a big kiss!"

"Now, now," Hainzl said laughing. "That would go down as trying to bribe a police officer. Let's just say the thought was there."

"Yes, that's a relief. Are we free to go now?" Brett asked.

"You are, and as a memory of your adventure here in Petra, you can keep the lamp you dug up. We've had it checked by one of the experts, and it's a very common variety actually worth very little." Passing a piece of paper across the desk he added, "Here is an export permit in case you are asked to show it."

With final words of thanks, the two of them happily returned to their car and drove back to the hotel.

"I can't believe it all worked out so well," Shirley said when she and Ralph heard the story. "It's been quite an adventure for all of us, but tomorrow we have to return home. At least all four of us will be on that plane." Turning to Vickie she added, "And you'll have achieved one of the main aims you came all this way for."

"Do tell me," Vickie asked.

"Why, to obtain another exhibit for your cabinet of curiosities, of course!"

King Cole

"That's another fine mess we've gotten ourselves into," His Majesty King Cole joked to his companion, echoing the comments that Oliver Hardy used to make to Stan Laurel. "All we can do now is wait until someone finds us – if they ever do."

They made themselves as comfortable as possible on the deserted beach, sheltering from the harsh sun under one of the few palm trees that broke up the endless expanse of sand. 'If only I hadn't suggested it', he kept repeating to himself, but that did nothing to help them out of their current situation. His thoughts went back over the events of the last few weeks.

The King had been entertaining a visiting ambassador at the palace. Having just finished eating a dinner that would have fed at least three men of normal girth, washed down with copious volumes of red wine, it was now time for them to sit back and be entertained by his musicians. "Bring me my pipe and bowl of tobacco," he instructed one of the servants. "And tell the fiddlers we're ready to hear them. They better be good, as I'm in no mood for a poor performance."

The musical trio entered and started to play, trying to hide their nervousness. At first he tapped his foot in time with the rhythm, and chatted with his guest. But the soporific effects of the food and drink soon started to take their toll, and his eyelids gradually lost their battle to remain open. He suddenly became aware the music had stopped and, with an effort, opened his eyes and looked around. "Why have you ceased playing?" he asked the fiddlers.

"Sire, we saw that you were asleep and didn't want to disturb your slumbers. After an hour we thought it best to stop. Would you like us to continue?"

"Of course I wasn't sleeping," he lied. "Just resting my eyes, but you may now depart."

He had been amused when the ambassador told him that he, the King, reminded him of Henry the Eighth. Although it was meant as a compliment, he was not convinced. He knew Henry was regarded as a charismatic monarch who did all sorts of jolly things. If you enjoyed eating, drinking, and generally larking about with the opposite gender, then he was your man. But dig a little deeper and you would learn that he was one of the cruellest and most destructive kings there had been in this country.

What had tickled him was hearing a group of children in the street singing a song they'd made up:

Old King Cole was a merry old soul, and a merry old soul was he.

Whilst he didn't care for the epithet 'old', he was pleased to be regarded as 'merry'. He didn't want to believe it when someone told him the song was not about him, but a cloth merchant called Old Thomas Cole who lived at the time of the first King Henry. Thomas used to stop off at a pub called 'The Ostrich' when he was travelling, not realising the proprietors were serial murderers. In one of the bedrooms they had rigged up a trapdoor that dropped wealthy guests into a vat of boiling water below. However, good fortune always intervened to prevent the amiable clothier becoming a victim.

"Your Majesty, it's getting late and we really must talk about the forthcoming visit of my Queen," the ambassador said, abruptly bringing the King back to the present.

"Oh, alright," he replied with some reluctance. "When can I expect her?"

"Sir, in two day's time she'll be at your palace by noon. She is new to the throne and is keen to form alliances with neighbouring countries. I know she would be pleased to stay for a few days and be shown the delights of your land."

"That leaves me little time to prepare," the King said, a touch of grumpiness invading his voice. "Pray tell me some more about her."

"She is Elizabeth of Bohemia, unmarried, and was thrust into Queenship by the sudden death of her uncle who left no descendents. Before that she made a good living baking cakes and selling them for a fair price."

Hearing this mention of food significantly increased his enthusiasm for the visit. "Would she be prepared to demonstrate her culinary expertise in the palace kitchen so that I can savour her creations for myself?" he asked.

"I'm sure she would be pleased to do so, Sir, if it serves to generate goodwill between your two countries. You may be amused to know that the people have composed a little rhyme about her:

The Queen of Hearts, she made some tarts, all on a summer's day."

"Please tell your Queen that she'll be most welcome, and that I'm looking forward to meeting her."

With that they each retired to their beds, but the King lay awake thinking about the royal visit. The Queen was single, and so was he; she obviously liked her food, and so did he. This could provide a very interesting diversion from the usual day-to-day palace routine.

He remembered how he felt on the day of the visit. The Queen's carriage drew up at the palace gates, and he waited expectantly as she alighted. Hmm, nice looking and not too old, he mused as she walked toward him. "Welcome to my humble abode, Your Highness," he said, bowing and then taking her hand. "I'm looking forward to our discussions, and showing you my country."

"That is most gracious of you, Sir," she replied, smiling sweetly and bobbing a curtsy. "It's an honour to meet you."

They went indoors, with the Queen's handmaid following with her luggage. Dinner that evening was another sumptuous affair, but this time the King was careful not to over indulge on the wine. Dining with a lady was a rare experience for him, and he wanted to remain sober so he could enjoy conversing with his comely guest. "You have a reputation of being an excellent baker," he said. "I would truly enjoy sampling some of your wares."

"It would be a pleasure to bake something for you," the Queen said. "And it would be a small token of my gratitude for your hospitality."

Their friendship blossomed over the next few days, and the Queen's tarts were enjoyed by all who tasted them. The King thought it might enhance their relationship even further if his guest was willing to join him on the royal yacht for a sail along his country's coastline. "Yes please," she replied. "I would enjoy a sea trip before I have to return home."

It had all started so well, he recalled. For two days a light wind propelled them along at a fair pace, but then came the storm. The captain and his small crew could not control the vessel, and it started taking on water. "Abandon ship!" he announced.

There was no time to collect any provisions before they all found themselves in the sea. The King managed to grab a large piece of driftwood, and then reached out for the Queen. Together they kicked out for the land they could just see through the spray, and eventually reached the beach, bedraggled and exhausted.

The storm passed as quickly as it had come, and the cloud was replaced by the blistering sun from which they now tried to shelter. "Are we the only survivors?" the Queen asked.

"I don't know," the King replied. "But we were not far from the shore when we went down, and others probably managed to reach it further along the coast." Feeling guilty that this pleasure trip had not turned out as he had anticipated, he felt compelled to add, "I'm truly sorry about what has happened. Rather than strengthen the ties between our two countries, I fear that it may have weakened them."

The Queen smiled. "Not at all; this was not of your making, and we are the stronger for having survived this unfortunate disaster. I'm sure a rescue boat will find us very soon. "Let's try and see the funny side of our situation. It didn't turn out to be a case of: *Row row row the boat, gently down the stream*," she sang. "But more like: *The waves in the sea go up and down, up and down*."

Delighted that his companion was not blaming him for the disaster, the King chortled, "But it would've been worse if we'd disappeared because: *There's a hole in the bottom of the sea, a hole in the bottom of the sea*!"

When the lifeboat crew arrived, rather than being greeted with cries of '*Off with their heads*,' they were relieved to find the royal couple singing and laughing. They were indeed merry old souls.

Afternoon Tea

I don't like queuing, as my wife will confirm, but here we are on a Saturday afternoon in August standing patiently in a line of people at our local upmarket garden centre restaurant. Last Christmas we'd been given an afternoon tea voucher by one of our sons but, like most eating places, this one had been closed for months because of the Covid-19 lockdown restrictions. However, today is the big day when we would finally spend it.

As the restaurant is so popular, customers can't book in advance but have to take their chance and be prepared to wait. We queued. Eventually we were shown to a table and placed our order – the standard afternoon tea for two, but no meat in the sandwiches. The pots of tea came fairly quickly; the food came half an hour later. Thus there was plenty of time to look around at our fellow customers, and it proves to be an interesting diversion.

The first thing I notice is that there are many tables with just two ladies sitting together. Without even turning my head I can see at least five examples of varying shapes and sizes. My wife explains that this is a popular venue for friends to meet for a morning coffee or lunch.

On a table next to a big glass sliding door that leads to an outside area displaying shrubs and garden ornaments sits a girl with bare shoulders and long hair. Opposite is her friend, who is wearing a patterned blouse and has her dark locks tied up in a bob on the top of her head. I wonder what they're saying to each other. As I can't lip read, I must use my imagination.

Bobbed Hair takes a drink from her cup. 'Did you sort out that rude teacher at your son's school? she asks.

'He thinks he's the bee's knees, and he accused our boy of trying to cheat during a test,' Bare Shoulders replies. 'When I collected him yesterday I went to the teacher and told him that David would never do such a thing, and he was very upset to have been picked out in front of the rest of the class like that.'

'What did the teacher say then?'

'Oh, he just mumbled something about he saw the lad looking at what the boy on the next desk was doing. But all the time he was talking the cheeky devil was trying to look down my cleavage.'

'Typical man,' Bobbed Hair snorts. 'Is he married? Is he good looking?'

'I did notice a wedding band on his finger, and he is rather dishy. Maybe he's starved of affection at home.'

'Or just a dirty, not-very-old, man.' They chuckle, and then remain silent for a time, no doubt preoccupied with their thoughts – or maybe it was the sight of the plate of yummy cakes the waitress had just put in front of them.

On a table next to ours sit another two young women. Actually, they just seem like girls to me but then so do all females under the age of forty.

The one facing us has long brown hair hanging down her back and is wearing a dark top. Turned half away from my gaze sits a mum-to-be, dressed in a spotted white blouse and blue trousers. She's making no attempt to hide her baby bump, and massages it frequently. My wife told me later that she was probably about six months pregnant, and that the baby was no doubt starting to move around. Like us they were waiting for their food to arrive, chatting merrily away whilst enjoying a cooling soft drink.

I can't hear what they're saying, and wouldn't have attempted to eaves drop even if I could. Perhaps their conversation started off on the subject of babies: 'How much longer to go before the big day' Long Hair asks.

'He's due three months today,' Mum-to-Be replies, giving her tummy another rub. 'I went for my postnatal check-up yesterday, and the nurse said there was no reason he wouldn't be on time.'

'That's good to hear. But I'd forgotten you already know the baby's sex. Did you ever consider just waiting to see what arrives, like many had to do before these scans were invented?'

Mum-to-Be adjusts the band that's holding her fair hair away from her face. 'Not really, but I can understand how all the family and friends used to be anxiously waiting to be told once the baby had arrived. Knowing it now means we can go ahead and buy the appropriate clothes and toys.'

'Oh yes, that'll be helpful,' Long Hair comments, but what she really wants to say is: 'What a load of nonsense; it's just being sexist. These days we treat all babies the same. When I have children I'll make sure they don't have a label stuck on them displaying whether they are girls or boys.'

'Have you fixed a date for your wedding?' Mum-to-Be asks. 'You must've been engaged for a year now.'

'No, not yet. He keeps saying we should wait a bit longer and build up some savings first.'

'But the time when you've enough money never comes. When we got married we had to buy some of our furniture from charity shops. We found some great bargains that way.'

Long Hair shakes her locks and displays a rather pained expression. 'Oh no, we wouldn't want to do that,' she says. 'We want to be able to move into our new home with everything just perfect. What would our friends say if they came to our house-warming party and saw second hand stuff? No I think we'll wait a bit.'

Silence followed.

My attention is diverted toward the afternoon tea that has finally arrived at our table. Let's see if it's worth the money our son paid for it. I take a photo, making sure I include some of the other customers in the background as an aid memoir for this account.

On the tray is a selection of sandwiches cut into quarters, and for each of us a small trifle in a glass jar, a jam tart topped with some cream and a strawberry, a slice of cake, and a fruit scone with jam and cream. Not bad, but my wife estimates that the actual value if you made it yourself to be about a quarter of what it cost here. But of course we didn't make it ourselves, and on this occasion we didn't pay for it. The restaurant has to cover overheads and make a profit, so the right thing to do was just eat, drink and be merry.

I look across to the Mum-to-Be and her friend. Their food has also appeared and one of them was having the most delicious looking 'super salad'. It is topped with several slices of avocado, and I make a mental note to order this the next time we visit. But I would resist impairing the healthy nature of this dish with a bowl of chips as the two ladies have done.

Once we'd satisfied our inner beings with all we could comfortably imbibe, there is the opportunity to look around again at our fellow diners. I notice two couples nearby where the romantic element is at work, or at least being cultivated. A man with an in-vogue shaven head displays a perpetual smile toward the woman sitting opposite him. His pale yellow shirt, open almost to the waist, reveals a gold neck chain that matches a similar ornament on his right wrist. Light blue trousers completes his wardrobe. I can only see the back of his companion, with her shoulder-length fair hair spread over her turquoise sweater.

To me the scenario is clear. Here is an older man on his best behaviour, dressed to impress a younger woman he has probably invited out for the first time. A safe option to test the water, meeting in a restaurant like this with many other customers present. The impression I have is that the poor woman may have had an unhappy experience and is glad to have the chance to talk about it. Superficially at least, her companion is trying to respond sensitively to her feelings and is working hard to say and do the right thing. The early signs suggest he is making some headway, but I feel like shouting out to her: 'Beware of wolves in sheep's clothing.'

'I'm sorry to hear what happened, my dear,' he could be saying. 'Do you want to tell me more about it?'

She appears to be responding; she talks, he listens, occasionally nodding, his smile never waning. Now and again he briefly stretches out his hand and lightly touches her knee. She doesn't seem to object. I look away and chat with my wife. Next time I glance, she has put her hand on *his* knee, and he is holding it. It looks like he's succeeded in snaring her. Sympathy can be a successful gambit, but I'm left hoping that his intentions are honourable. Poor girl, I'm guessing she has been let down once already, and it would be tragic if her apparent confidence in this lothario ends in another disaster.

Sitting nearby is a younger couple. They seem slightly incongruous among the older members of the community who make up most of the clientele. His clothing is dark and his head betrays a recent trip to the barbers to obtain a currently fashionable short hair cut. Looking at him is a blond girl with glasses, sporting a light green top. For the whole time we are there all they order is a coffee for him and a fruit drink for her. It seems a tad inconsiderate to be holding up a table when other customers are still queuing to spend much more money than they are doing.

There looks to be quite an intense and serious conversation taking place. It's different from that of the other couple – there are no smiles and little body language, and this time it is the man who's doing most of the talking. No, not a first date, I surmise. It looks more like he may have done something wrong and is now trying to make amends. Maybe he's saying, 'I'm really sorry I went off with that other girl and left you in the lurch.' She listens but doesn't immediately respond.

'I promise I won't do that again. Can you please just give me another chance?'

His pleas must have eventually born fruit as, just before we leave, I did see his hand go across the table and she gently touched it. Ah well, young love has its own challenges, and maybe that meeting on neutral ground triggered a new chapter in their relationship.

We wrap up the uneaten two slices of cake and stand up to go. As we pass their table, I can't resist commenting to the Mum-to-Be how delicious her super salad looks. She agrees that it is, and her companion says she's jealous even though what she had ordered for herself was also good.

We look forward to our next visit when we can continue our pastime of people watching, and I know what I'll be ordering from the menu. But the jury is still out on whether or not it will include a bowl of chips!

Puppy Love

"Have you seen Valerie's new dog?" Margaret asked Jane as they walked in through the high school gates on a cold Monday morning.

"No, didn't know she had another one to train," Jane replied, tucking her scarf tighter around her neck to keep out the biting wind.

"Their last one, Bruno, went off to Guide Dogs for advanced training a few weeks ago, after completing the basic programme. Her parents said they were happy to take in another one."

"It must be hard having to say goodbye to a dog you've loved and cared for during the last year or more," Jane commented.

"Yes, it must," agreed Margaret. "I believe they usually arrive when they're only six or seven weeks old. We'll have to ask Val how she managed to cope with losing Bruno."

All thoughts of dogs faded as the girls went into their classes. It was their final year, and examinations were looming. But, once the bell had rung to signal school was over for the day, Margaret quickly sought out Valerie.

"Hi Val. Jane and I were wondering just what it was like to lose Bruno. I often saw you out walking with him when he was wearing that training harness. You must've grown very fond of him."

"It was hard, but of course I was expecting it," replied Valerie. "We know he'll go to a good home and help somebody who urgently needs a pair of eyes to keep them safe. Would you like to come round and meet our new arrival?"

"Oh yes please," Margaret said. "But I'll just check with Jane first. When would be a good time?"

"Let's make it next Saturday morning; you don't want to be going out at night in this weather."

As they set off to walk back home, Margaret updated Jane on the invitation to see Val's new puppy. The boy's high school was next to theirs, and usually some of the lads waited by the gate to eye the girls as they walked past. The more brazen lads used to call out cheeky comments like, "Hi beautiful, want to come over here for a cuddle?" or

"Where have you been all my life, darling?" Although the girls always pretended to be uninterested in these ribald utterances, they were nevertheless making furtive glances sideways to see whom they fancied.

I like that quiet one with the dark hair, standing on his own," Margaret said. "I've noticed him before; he's always smiling but never says anything. One of these days I'm going to stop and ask him his name."

"Well why don't you do it now?" Jane suggested. "Otherwise, before you know it, he'll have disappeared."

Egged on by her friend, Margaret sauntered toward the boy, turned her head in his direction and smiled. His eyes brightened. "Hello," he said. Should she stop and speak with him? Jane obviously thought so, and deliberately stood in front of her friend so she couldn't continue onwards.

"Oh hello," Margaret replied, trying to make it sound like it was just a superficial acknowledgement.

"I'm sorry my schoolmates are embarrassing all you girls with their shouting; it's very rude of them."

"Oh we don't mind, it's all a bit of fun really."

"Glad you're not offended. My name's Brian."

Unusual for a lad to be so polite, thought Margaret, but he does look a year or two older than the others so perhaps he's learned a bit of sense. "I'm Margaret and my friend here is Jane."

"Hi Jane. Are you both on your way to the bus stop?"

"No, we only live fifteen minutes away, so we walk," Jane replied.

Margaret didn't want him to think they were trying to be too familiar. "Right, Brian, we'd better be on our way. Maybe see you around some time."

"Now don't say you don't like him," Jane said when they were out of earshot. "I could see the glint in your eye."

"Okay, maybe you're right, but let's leave it at that for now. We've our homework to think about, and then going to Valerie's on Saturday to see her new puppy."

Now that the ice had been broken, or at least cracked just a little, Margaret was hoping that Brian would be outside his school the next day, but it was raining and Jane's father came to take them home in his car. It was dry on Wednesday, and sure enough he was there at his usual spot.

He waved to the two girls when he saw them approaching.

"Hi Brian, how was your day?" Margaret asked casually.

"A bit boring at times, but I always enjoy the biology lessons. How was yours?"

But Jane interrupted. "I'm going to walk on ahead and leave you two to chat," she said, trying to suppress one of those looks that hinted she was aware of where this innocent conversation could lead.

"Oh, alright, I'll catch up with you in a moment." But, by the time she had discovered that Brian was hoping to become a veterinary surgeon, and had revealed her own interest in animals, her friend was out of sight.

The time spent chatting increased as the week wore on, but then came Saturday and the opportunity for her and Jane to see Valerie's new dog. "My goodness, isn't he gorgeous!" Margaret exclaimed as soon as she set eyes on the puppy. What breed is he?"

"He's a golden retriever, and just eight weeks old now."

"But he's so small compared with Bruno you had before. Have you thought of a name for him yet?"

"The only thing we could think of in view of his size is 'Tiny', but of course he'll also have his posh pedigree name."

After the three girls had enjoyed running around playing with the puppy for half an hour, Valerie said, "There'll be a dog show in the middle of February, held in the church hall. One category is for animals younger than three months, and we're thinking of entering Tiny for this."

"What does a dog have to do at this age, apart from look pretty?" Jane asked.

"You're right about looking good and well groomed, but they need to have learned at least two commands. We're teaching him to sit and stay when told to, and then come when he's called."

"We must come and see how you get on, but it's the first of the month tomorrow so you only have a couple of weeks to teach him these tricks," said Margaret. "Anyway, we must be moving on. Thanks for letting us see this lovely little chap, and good luck with the training."

Monday came all too quickly, and life for the girls resumed its routine of school, homework and family meals. It took Margaret a little while to recognise that the highlight of the day had become the chats she had with

Brian on the way home. Jane had given up waiting for her friend, and just left her to make her own way home.

By the end of the second week, Margaret started to wonder if she should suggest meeting the young man away from the school. He'd not mentioned it, and she worried if it would make her

look pushy if she raised this herself. Plucking up courage she said, "Brian, my friend Valerie is entering her new puppy in a dog show at the church on Sunday afternoon. Do you fancy coming along to watch?"

"Sounds a great idea; I'd love to be there. Thanks for telling me."

Margaret made an effort not to appear pleased, and just replied, "Okay, fine. Maybe see you there then."

Sunday could not come soon enough. What should she wear? Not her best clothes, that would be a bit obvious. It was a dog show after all, so something casual would do. By the time she and Jane arrived at the hall, Valerie was already there, registering Tiny for the puppy event. Margaret looked around. No sign of Brian. Had he decided not to come after all?

The events for adult dogs started. The judges firstly examined the condition of the entries and then marked the score cards as they went through their various commands. Eventually, it was time for the juvenile event. But then Margaret saw Brian coming toward them. "So sorry I'm late, ladies," he said, sounding breathless. "Firstly I had to go and buy something, and then I went down the wrong street for the church hall."

Margaret felt her heart give a flutter. "Glad you could make it, Brian. You already know Jane, but this is my friend Valerie and her puppy, Tiny."

"Nice to meet you," Brian said. "Good luck with competition."

"I see the judging is just about to begin," interrupted Margaret. "Yes good luck, Val, we'll keep everything crossed."

"Thanks. It looks like we're on second."

"Nice condition, this one," the judge commented after he had examined Tiny. "Okay, show me what he can do."

The little pup performed perfectly, staying just where he was until called. The judge made a note on his card and just said, "Thank you," before moving on to the next entry.

"What do you think, Val?" said Jane. "It looks like your little friend did well."

"Maybe, but it'll depend on the other contestants. We'll just have to wait and see what the judge announces."

It was an anxious few minutes. Then the judge came over to Valerie with a card in his hand. "Congratulations," he said. "Your puppy has won first prize." The little group were unable to suppress a spontaneous cheer.

Margaret felt something was being put into her hand. Looking down, she saw it was a little box containing a red rose.

Brian was smiling at her. "Do you realise it's February the fourteenth, and it's . . .

Val-and-Tiny's Day!"

I am Melchizedek

My name is Melchizedek, but who am I? I came to explore your world more than four thousand of your Earth years ago and decided to stay for a while. Nobody saw me arrive, but I came the same way as did other visitors did from my world. And what was this way? you are probably asking.

Many instances of what to you were mysterious happenings were included in your religious writings, and anything you don't understand is still often attributed to the actions of a deity you call God. This was more common in my early days when your knowledge of science was even more primitive than it is now.

When one of my countrymen landed, an observer of yours wrote in a book you call *Exodus,* 'The whole of Mount Sinai was covered with smoke, because the Lord descended on it in fire . . . the whole mountain trembled violently.' Then, when another decided to leave, someone wrote in your *Second Book of Kings*, 'Suddenly a chariot of fire and horses of fire appeared . . . and Elijah went up to heaven in a whirlwind.'

It was less than a hundred years ago that you invented rockets but, had any of my people arrived since then, you would have recognised the form of transport that brought them here. Your primitive ancestors had no understanding of these machines, so they could only describe the events in terms of horses, chariots and whirlwinds.

During my first few years with you I met many folk and was happy to help them with their challenges. I even advised Pharaoh Djoser on how to construct the first pyramid. Some of your texts mention me by name, but the references are only brief. Perhaps it was assumed I was so well known that it was unnecessary to describe me in detail. Before I reveal who I really am, I shall review for you what has been written about me.

One of the people I met was your prophet Abraham, and this received a mention in your book *Genesis*. It states that I visited him after he had been victorious in battle, and that I was a king and high priest. I gave him food and wine; in return he gave me a tenth of his spoils of war. Nothing else is said about me there, although I must have been famous to have Abraham give me the tithes.

A thousand years later your King David cited me in his *Psalm* number 110. He wrote that his lord would be 'a priest forever in the order of

Melchizedek'. Once again he clearly did not feel the need to state why this was so significant, which does pose an enigma for those who wish to know more about me. Yet still another millennia after that, your religious book *Hebrews* refers to the figure of Jesus as being a 'high priest, in line of succession to Melchizedek.' This was intended to mean that he was not from the usual line of priests, but from one of an altogether higher level – a successor to me! This is very flattering, but is it justified?

When other scholars failed to discover accounts of my early years, they sometimes became fanciful and let their imaginations fill in the gaps. Two thousand years after my arrival, one clearly frustrated researcher in Egypt wrote *The Book of the Secrets of Enoch*. In it, he stated that my parents were Nir, the brother of Noah, and his wife Sopanima, but it seems that my creation was not the result of a union between them. The author does not elaborate, but leaves the door open for an immaculate conception. His story relates that my mother died, but I nevertheless emerged from her womb not as a helpless baby but as a three-year old infant wearing clothes and able to speak!

Enoch weaves quite a story, because he continues by stating that I had the badge of priesthood on my breast. Oh dear, the scaly skin and possibly even horns and a tail would have made me look more like your idea of a devil than a king. He also wrote that I'd be taken by Archangel Michael to the Garden of Eden as a place of safety when the rest of the world was covered by the flood. Yes, I did visit the garden before it too disappeared under the waves, but I was able to find my own way there. Flying angels are just another example of myths that you people make up when you don't understand the true facts.

It was with great excitement when, in your year 1947, you discovered the Dead Sea Scrolls at Qumran. You deduced they were written a hundred years before what you call the Christian Era. This time I was depicted as an angel who would carry out the vengeance of your God, and free the people from the hand of evil spirits.

Another discovery you made around this time was a collection of texts buried in the sand at Nag Hammadi in Egypt. These were written a couple of hundred years after the Scrolls, and again mention that I am 'the Priest of the God Most High' and that I destroyed my enemies.

Although my name is also cited in some of your Jewish Midrashim commentaries, I shall just mention one other source where I appear, this time in a little more detail but not necessary accuracy. It is entitled *The Book of the Bee*, which has a whole chapter devoted to me. The author was Solomon of Akhlat. He lived three thousand years after I arrived, so the opportunity to interview eyewitnesses would have been limited!

Either he relied on his imagination, or obtained information from oral and written traditions that are now lost. Although he states that the names of my parents were not recorded, he still names them. Whereas Enoch had written that my father was Nir, the brother of Noah, this author says it was Noah's great-great grandson, Mâlâh. He adds that my mother was not Sopanima, but Yôzâdâk.

The scenario then somehow jumps forward a couple of millennia, and I was taken by Noah's son Shem to the place where Jesus was crucified. After that I was delivered to the priesthood and told to dwell there until the end of my life. Shem then returned to my parents and told them I had died and had been buried there. Enoch concludes his account by stating that in later life I became famous and eleven kings built Jerusalem for me.

Well, dear reader, this ends my review of the texts that have mentioned me, many of which are decidedly fanciful. So who really am I? There is much I cannot reveal because you are yet too immature to truly understand. But many years ago my people were much like you are now. We developed rockets for interplanetary travel, just like you have done. Our quest was to see if life had developed anywhere else, but our expeditions to our own neighbouring worlds failed to reveal any evidence of this.

We then discovered the ability to travel faster than the speed of light, which enabled us to visit neighbouring stars and even galaxies. You will have to discover this technology for yourself, and be mature enough to use it wisely. We searched far and wide, but the only other inhabited world we have yet discovered is your own. Because our two civilisations may be unique in the universe, we each have a responsibility to avoid destroying ourselves.

As my world is more advanced than yours, it behoves my people to exercise particular care in our dealings with you. You must be left to evolve at your own rate and not be suddenly presented with knowledge and technology beyond your ability to use it sensibly and wisely. I can understand now how I was perceived as a superior being, and perhaps I revealed too many of my powers too quickly.

Yes I was indeed present at the time of Noah, so your writers were correct in associating me with that noble family. But I was not a progeny of them, and I certainly didn't enter their lives as a three-year old child! In my world we have moved beyond the stage of fighting and killing each other in order to settle our differences. Yet one of the first things I heard about on my arrival here was the conflict involving your spiritual leader Abraham that I mentioned earlier.

During my stay on Earth there have been many wars, twelve of them before your Christian Era, and so far more than a hundred and twenty-five since then. Will you people never learn to live peacefully and settle your differences without resorting to killing each other? I have tried to intervene by entering the minds of some of your holy men and women, and encouraging them to preach peace and goodwill to all. But many of you have not listened, preferring to continue with your barbaric ways.

There is little more I can do to help you avoid self-destruction and leaving my own world alone as the sole harbinger of life. I shall leave you now, but will return at some time in the future to see if you have become more civilised. If you have sufficiently matured, I will make myself known and share some of my knowledge with you so that we can become neighbours. Should you continue as you are now, you will remain in isolation for as long as the universe exists.

Remember the Fifth

As he scrubbed his hands, rinsed them and turned off the tap with his elbow, Stephen Rigby was starting to feel the tension. He dried his hands on the disposable paper towels and donned the sterilised green surgical cap to cover his short brown hair. Was it usual for self doubt to creep in at this stage?

Perhaps talking about it would steady his nerves. "Dr Kahn, how did you feel when you carried out your first operation as an intern?"

"I felt nervous, Stephen," the consultant replied, but I was confident my training and many sessions as an assistant would see me through."

"Thanks, I'm quite relieved to hear it's not just me who feels a bit nervy at times like this. I've assisted you more times than I can remember, but this time *I* perform the surgery and you formally assess me."

"It's just part of the training before you can graduate as a fully qualified doctor. We've all been through this part of the assessment, and I'm sure you'll be fine," Kahn said.

"I'll certainly do my best," Stephen replied. But he knew that, without a satisfactory report from his superior, he would have to repeat a whole year of his training.

The pair completed their sanitisation procedures, pulled on latex gloves and face masks, and started to walk through to the operating theatre. As they proceeded in silence, Stephen's mind went back to his first day at medical school. He had worked so hard to obtain a place there – science at advanced level, volunteer work in hospitals, applications to half a dozen universities. One rejection followed another until, shortly after his twenty-first birthday, the letter came. The whole family went out for a celebratory dinner that same evening.

He remembered how demanding the training was. Yet more science, then so much anatomy that he could soon name every bone and muscle in the body without even pausing for breath. Then came pharmacology, psychology, pathology, and even more 'ologies.' Such a lot of theory, but he was not allowed to be anywhere near a patient.

Perhaps I was lucky in passing all those tests and exams, Stephen said to himself. But things became much more interesting when, during the third year. Along with other students, he accompanied consultants on their hospital rounds and clinics. Still no touching of patients, but the experience gained from watching and listening during real medical procedures added dynamism to the theory he had soaked up during the previous two years.

Now, after a total of nearly seven years of learning and assisting, he had fulfilled all the requirements for the medical half of the degree. All that remained before he could be awarded the title of doctor was to prove his worth with the surgical portion. If he was to avoid repeating this final year, he must do well today to ensure that Dr Kahn could send a satisfactory report to the examination board.

As they reached the door of the operating theatre, he was quickly jolted out of his musings by the sound of a friendly voice. It was Dr Marjory Langley, the anaesthetist, who'd arrived there before them. From the crinkles at the corner of her eyes it was clear she was smiling behind her mask. "Good morning Ajmal." Dr Kahn nodded. "Morning, Stephen. How are you feeling?"

"Hi Dr Langley, good to see you. Just a bit nervous, thanks."

"We've all been through this first time; I'm sure you'll do well. If anything goes wrong, just remember the five rights of medical administration." Her helpful advice and reassurance sounded almost motherly.

"Thank you. These directives are engraved on my brain, even if I forget what day it is," Stephen said, trying to let a bit of jocularity help calm his nerves.

"Is the patient on his way?" Dr Kahn asked the senior theatre sister.

"Sorry about the delay, doctor. Mr Wilkinson was in pain early this morning. He had to be given some medication before he could be made ready for the surgery. I'm expecting him any minute now."

Impatient though Stephen was to begin, the short wait gave him time to mentally rehearse the five rights that Dr Langley had mentioned. To reduce medication errors, one must firstly confirm it's the right patient, secondly that it's the right drug, thirdly that it's the right dose, and fourthly that it's the right route. Now what was number five? He couldn't remember. It was like trying to name six of the seven dwarves and forgetting the last one. Hopefully it would come back to him should he need it.

All further musings came to a halt with the arrival of the patient. Seventy five-year old John Wilkinson was here for investigative surgery to find the cause of his persistent abdominal discomfort. The scans had indicated there could be a growth constricting part of his colon, but it was impossible to give a firm diagnosis without surgical intervention. If only this could have been a straight forward appendectomy, as some of his fellow interns had been faced with, Stephen thought.

He helped lift the patient onto the operating table, and then stood back whilst Dr Langley commenced the anesthetising procedure. "Are you ready, Stephen?" Dr Kahn asked. "The patient is now fully asleep and is being monitored, so you can start when you wish."

So the moment had finally arrived. With his supervisor watching from a short distance, Stephen selected a scalpel and made an incision in the patient's abdomen. "Swabs!" he called out, and pressed them down on the wound to stem the blood flow. "Retractors!" he pulled back the skin to expose the organs lying beneath. So far so good, he thought. Now let me just locate what it is that's causing the trouble.

He gently felt his way along the colon. "Ah, here's the culprit!" he announced to all within earshot. "There's a lump pressing down on the bowel. Difficult to tell if it's cancerous or just a benign tumour. I shall take a biopsy for the lab to analyse."

The consultant had been content to leave Stephen to carry out his task, and saw no reason to intervene. He was glad to see his student appeared to have settled down, now that he was fully engaged with his work. Just as he was about to make some complimentary comment, a nurse opened the door. "Dr Kahn, there's an urgent telephone call from the intensive care ward. One of your patients from this morning has just collapsed. Can you come?"

"Give me a moment," he shouted back. "Stephen, what do you still intend to do with this patient?"

"I've now taken the biopsy, but don't think I should try to excise the obstruction until we have the lab result. My proposal is to close the wound and insert clamps over it to keep it closed until we have the report."

"Alright, I agree with your decision. If all you have to do now is close the wound, would you be confident if I left you to it so I can quickly attend to my own patient?"

"Of course, doctor, I should be finished in another ten minutes."

Dr Kahn quickly left the theatre, and Stephen commenced closing the wound.

A few moments later, without warning, Dr Langley shouted: "The patient's vital signs have suddenly deteriorated. We may lose him. I've just turned off the anaesthetic and am commencing cardiopulmonary resuscitation. You must quickly do what is necessary to revive him."

Stephen realised it was now up to him to save the patient. He would administer an intracardiac injection of adrenalin. "Please fetch the emergency equipment," he instructed the theatre sister. This was when he needed to follow the 'five rights of medication administration.' The right patient; yes. The right drug, adrenaline; yes. The right dose; yes. The right route, intracardiac; yes. Now what was the fifth?

The moment the nurse handed him the syringe, Stephen drew in the adrenaline and inserted the needle through the space between the fourth and fifth ribs.

"Stop!" Dr Langley shouted. But it was too late; he had already pressed the plunger and injected the drug directly into the patient's heart.

"What are you doing?" the anaesthetist bellowed. "He's now going into distress and I don't think I can save him."

"I just gave him an intracardiac injection of adrenaline, as we're taught to do," Stephen replied, now starting to panic.

"You know this should not be done during CPR. I told you not to forget the five rights; but you've just ignored the last one."

At last it came to Stephen. Not only must it be the right patient, drug, dose, and route, but it also had to be at the *right time*. If only he had remembered, remembered the fifth.

The Game

"Please do you have something more valuable you can give me in exchange for these paper tissues and a pen?" With an effort Simon opened his eyes, closed to protect them from the bright afternoon sun – or at least that's the excuse he gave himself for nodding off on the park bench. He looked up to see a young lady proffering him a small pack of paper tissues and a cheap ball-point pen.

The fish and chip lunch he and his wife Claire had enjoyed at the seafront cafe was still exerting a soporific effect on his concentration. "I don't understand. Do you want me to buy these from you?

"Oh no. Sorry, I don't want money," she said. "I better explain. My name is Jenna and I'm with a party of overseas students here on holiday. Our tutor has given us a task to do this afternoon. We have to start with a cheap object and then try and exchange it for something more valuable. Then we keep doing this to see who can end up with the most valuable item after two hours. The winner gets a prize."

"Ah, I see, it's a game, a test of your initiative," Simon replied, nudging his wife to make sure she was awake. "Claire, what do you think? Do we have anything we could swap for these items?

Claire rummaged around in her handbag which, as one might expect from an experienced holidaymaker, contained all the items needed to sustain the average couple for a month or more. "Will this do?" she asked, extracting from its depths, in the manner of a magician pulling a rabbit out of a hat, a folded shopping bag in its little pouch.

Jenna looked at it for moment, wondering if she should accept this offer. "Thank you. I think it should be worth more than what I have already, if you're sure you can spare it."

"Don't worry, I do have another one, and we'd like you to have a chance of winning."

"Thanks again," Jenna said as she handed over the tissues and pen to Claire and took the shopping bag from her. She scampered off to find another victim, buoyed on by good luck exhortations from her first patrons.

"I wonder what she'll end up with, and also the other students," Claire mused, as much as a reflection as a question.

"Probably nothing very valuable from a group of holidaymakers like us," Simon replied.

"Maybe a pair of sun glasses or an item of cheap jewellery. If anyone is to part with a more expensive item, they'll need to be offered something they really want."

"I'm not sure about that. If you're a long way from a shop and dying for a drink in this hot sun, then an unopened bottle of water may tempt you to exchange it for something that cost a lot more."

"Good point," Simon conceded. "Value does depend on more than how many pennies you have to pay for something. Do you remember reading about a man who started out just like these youngsters are doing, and ended up with a perfectly useable motor vehicle?"

Claire laughed. "That was just a freak example; most people who try this will end up with less than they started with."

Simon now had the bit between his teeth. "But determination in life will take you a long way, and these kids we're watching this afternoon are learning an important lesson. Full marks to their teacher for selecting this task."

"Well, maybe," his wife replied. "But I'd rather just save up to buy what I need than go to all that trouble."

"D'you know, I think I might give this a go. Now that I'm retired I need a challenge. When we return home I'm going to do it."

Claire adopted that tolerant but disbelieving air that parents use with children when they come to them with wild ideas. "Okay, what are you going to aim for then?"

"We've always said how great it would be to have a boat on the canal," Simon said without hesitating. "It always looks so leisurely and peaceful when we see them down at our local marina. That'll be my target."

"But those converted canal barges cost a fortune! Some people actually live on them permanently."

"No, no. I wasn't thinking about those house boats; just a modest little cabin cruiser so we can spend a couple of hours chugging up and down when the weather is fine."

"Well, if you're set on it, the best of luck," Claire replied with an air of resignation. "You can't resist buying those cheap watches, where the replacement battery costs more than you paid in the first place. Why not start by offering one of those?"

"Ah, I knew you'd begin to share my enthusiasm sooner or later, and thanks for your suggestion," Simon said gleefully. "As soon as we get home I'll fish out one that's still working."

With that, they remained quiet and continued their people watch from the comfort of the park bench. The sun still shone brightly, and once again they found it difficult to keep their eyes open. The gentle sound of their snoring was lost amidst the playful shouts of the children and their parents trying to keep them under control.

* * *

Perhaps it's unusual to look forward to being back home when you're enjoying a holiday, but the thought of owning his own little boat dominated Simon's thoughts during the rest of their stay. Once they'd safely returned to their semi-detached house in the Midlands, he left his wife to sort out the inevitable pile of washing and went to look at his watch collection. 'Do I really want to let one of these go?' He asked himself. But Clare was right, there are too many. 'Here's one I bought last year for ten pounds; it's still going and I can't remember the last time I wore it. It'll do'.

"Unless you need me for anything, I think I'll meet the lads for a round of golf tomorrow," he said to his wife as she was loading the washing machine.

"Oh, there'll only be all the ironing to do before I start to prepare lunch," she replied, knowing that he would be more of a hindrance than a help if he hung around when she was trying to get things done. "You could always do it for me whilst I put my feet up and enjoy a cup of coffee?"

"I'd love to, but remember how the last time I tried to iron I got the creases in all the wrong places," he said, conscious of the fact that he could have done a proper job if he had made the effort.

"Yes, I remember, and I had to do it all over again myself. Perhaps you'd be better out of the way after all," Claire responded, not blind to her husband's deviousness little ruse.

Simon waited until his foursome had reached the third tee before taking the watch out of his pocket saying, "D'you know, I have too many watches. Anyone interested in taking this one from me?"

"That's a coincidence," his friend Bill said. "Mine's just given up the ghost. Let's have a look at it. Okay, it's not exactly a Rolex but it'll do for now. How much do want for it?"

'This is going to be easier than I imagined', Simon thought. "Actually, I must confess that I'm engaged in a swapping exercise. Do you have anything you could exchange for it?"

Bill considered for a moment before drawing a club from his golf bag. "Well, I do have this spare putter that I used before buying a better one. Is it any good for you?"

Simon didn't hesitate. "I'll take it if you're happy to make the swap."

"If I'd known you had a putter available, I'd have asked for it myself." This was Gordon, another of the foursome, who had been quietly following the exchanges.

"Oh, so sorry, Simon said. "I thought you already had a full set of clubs."

"No, it's not for me but for my twelve-year-old," Gordon replied. "I spent forty quid on a games console for him at Christmas, but he now says he's bored with it and just wants a decent putter of his own so he can go and play crazy golf with his mates."

"How about swapping me the games console for the putter?" Simon asked.

"Sounds good to me, as we were just going to take it to a charity shop. If you want to follow me home after we've finished here, you can have it."

"You're a bit late back," Claire said when Simon arrived home for lunch. "Have you been drinking again?"

"Sorry, love. No booze but I had to call at Gordon's house on the way back to pick up something."

"And just what was that?"

"This games console. Now before you start asking what we are going to do with it, I'll explain."

His wife listened quietly whilst Simon recounted the morning's events. "So you see," he concluded, "I now have something worth four times the value of my watch after just two exchanges. If I keep doubling up like this we'll soon have our cabin cruiser!"

"I'll believe that when I see it," Claire said. "But, by coincidence, I had Mary Jones around for coffee this morning and she mentioned that her young son keeps nagging them for a games console, claiming that all his friends have one."

"How interesting. I wonder if they'd have anything to exchange for this one."

"Well," she told me they'd bought him a guitar and even paid for him to have lessons, but he just didn't have the interest to practise. I'll give Mary a call after lunch."

Two hours later, Simon had the guitar. He checked online to find that it would have cost about eighty pounds new. It had been a successful day, he thought; almost too easy.

But he soon discovered that the next step was proving to be more difficult – nobody seemed interested in his newly acquired musical instrument. "Why don't you just advertise in the local paper, and specifically state you're looking for an exchange and not cash," Claire suggested after a couple of days of frustration and disappointment for Simon.

"I'm surprised by the number of responses I've received," Simon said a week later. "One of the callers has a decent bicycle he can no can no longer use after undergoing knee surgery. I'm taking the guitar round to his house right now."

"That worked out well for both of us," he commented when he arrived home pushing the bike. "I think I'll try the same trick with this."

"Maybe you should just enjoy riding the bicycle instead of chasing after a boat," Claire suggested. "You've done very well to say you started off with a cheap watch, so why not stop now when you're winning?"

"It just makes me more determined to press on," he said. "But I know that it might end in failure."

Claire adopted that look of resignation that only the fair sex can do well. "It's your decision so long as you don't spend our savings. I just hope you won't be upset if it doesn't work out."

A month later Simon summarised his progress to his wife. "I've managed to double the value with each exchange. First the watch, then the putter, games console, guitar, and bicycle. Then I swapped that for the self-propelled lawn mower, followed by the computer and then the smart television. I reckon its value is over a thousand pounds, so I now need something that costs twice as much. Any ideas?"

"There is a possibility," Claire said, surprised that he had achieved so much but still doubtful that his luck would hold.

"Do tell."

"You remember poor Colin who tragically lost his wife a few months back, and she was younger than me?"

"Yes, it's so sad."

"Well, he gave her a diamond ring for their silver wedding. He said it was an investment as well as a gift, as the value of the stones continues to rise. But he doesn't want to keep it any more now that his wife has gone."

"Thanks for the tip," Simon said. "Let's ask him round for a drink and I'll raise the matter in a casual way. Perhaps he might be interested in the smart TV; it does have all the gadgets built in."

"The diamond dealer confirms the three stones in the ring are worth at least a couple of thousand," Simon cheerfully reported a week later. "Now to see what I can exchange for them."

"I hope you're not going to ride that motorbike at your age," Claire said when she saw it being off-loaded outside their house. "It looks to be a powerful beast."

"No dear, I'm just keeping it in the garage until I can swap it for a car."

Her only response was a "humph".

"You were probably right all along, Claire," Simon said despondently a month later. "It looks like my grandiose idea might have run its course. Nobody seems to want the motorbike. Perhaps I should just try to sell it. At least we can then treat ourselves with the money I get for it."

"It's not like you to give up," Claire responded, now feeling a bit guilty that she had not been exactly encouraging her husband. "You achieved a lot in a short time, so why not keep going for a week or two at least before abandoning your dream."

"Thanks love. Okay, I'll just try for one more month before getting rid of the bike, but I'm not very optimistic of reaching the finishing line with this crazy stunt."

* * *

"I might have known you were up to something when you were so keen to swap that putter," Bill said after Simon had updated his golfing friends at the nineteenth hole after their morning's round. "But I admire you for sticking to your guns."

"Thanks mate, but do any of you know someone who would like a powerful motorbike in exchange for a car? It doesn't have to be a big one."

"I might do," Gordon piped up. "A friend of mine is a bit of a petrol head. He already has two cars and told me he would like to replay his misspent youth. A bike like you describe would enable him to race up and down like a maniac."

"Sounds good," Simon replied. Can you please give him my telephone number and ask him to call me if he wants to discuss a deal?"

"I'm so glad you encouraged me to keep going, Claire," Simon said to his wife when he arrived home in the car he had just acquired.

"To be honest, I did doubt you would get this far, but you've proved me wrong," she replied, this time not hiding her admiration for what her husband had achieved. "But do you still think you can take that final step?"

Simon beamed. "We can drive down to Marina tomorrow, just to see what's on sale."

* * *

"There is one possibility," the office manager said, after they'd looked at the various craft tied up on the moorings.

"Which is that?" Simon asked.

"One of my customers has a 28-foot cabin cruiser, complete with toilet and fridge, he's been trying to sell. It's thirty years old but still in good condition."

"How much does he want for it?"

"He was asking £15,000 but it's been sitting here for months now. I think he wants the money to buy a second-hand car."

"Can you perhaps call him and say I might be interested in discussing a possible deal?" Simon said, trying to conceal his mounting anticipation that the target might actually be in sight.

* * *

"Well, what do you think of it?" Simon asked Claire as they stepped on board *Little Princess*.

"It feels good, and I'm really proud of you," she said, giving her husband a hug. "I can't wait to begin our first cruise."

"Okay, let's cast off," he said, starting the engine. "I just need to untie this mooring rope and we're away." He lent over the side, and heard a splash. "Damn it! My watch has just dropped into the water. When we get back I'll have to go to the supermarket and buy another."

Claire's screamed response was muffled by the noise from the engine!

Shore Leave

"Have you managed to get through yet?" Mark Keeley asked the radio operator.

"No, sorry, still nothing but static," Steve replied. "These winter storms in the North Sea sometimes last for days."

"If this one does, the helicopter won't be able to take me back to base today. It's already late in the afternoon, and I've been stuck on this god dam oil rig for three weeks now. I need my shore leave."

"Yeah, I know how you feel," Steve said. "But you're lucky you don't have my job with a contract that stipulates double the time away from home than yours does."

Mark used both hands to smooth his dark hair that had been tousled by the wind. "But you just sit here all day playing with your radio," he replied. "I work twelve hours at a time joining pipes and repairing equipment."

Steve laughed. "Okay, I wouldn't want to get my hands dirty with your roustabout job, but I would like to go home to my family more often than I do. This is your first spell on a rig but I was posted to this one in 1973. My leave has been delayed umpteen times in the two years I've been here."

"That doesn't make me feel any happier," Mark said. "Can you please try again, as I'd really like to make a personal call to my home. I told Margaret I'd let her know when to expect me back, and she'll be worrying because she hasn't heard from me for three days. It's my first posting and she won't understand that these delays happen."

Steve adjusted his microphone. "This is *Ocean Giant* calling base. Come in please." Once again his request was met only with hissing and crackling from the speaker. "I'll try different frequencies including the emergency channel," he said, adjusting the tuning knobs and repeating his call sign. "No luck, I'm afraid, but I'll keep at it and let you know if I make contact so you can arrange that call."

Mark returned to his small cabin, opened a can of beer and lay on his bunk. I wonder what Margaret and little Charlie are doing now, he thought. It's Friday and they'll be expecting to see me at home tonight.

They're probably wondering why I haven't called to confirm. This is the first time I've left them alone for so long; I do hope they are alright. He took a few mouthfuls of his drink, and thought back over the previous few months.

Life had been good when he'd been working for the construction company near home, receiving a regular wage. But then it had closed down and he'd been out of a job at the age of thirty. The Job Centre suggested he apply for work on an oil rig in the North Sea, as the money was good for someone like me without professional qualifications. The only disadvantage was being away from home. When he'd discussed it with Margaret he remembered she hadn't been too happy, but it was either that or the soup kitchen.

So there he was. He did miss her, and playing with Charlie when he comes back from nursery school. Maybe when he got home – if he ever did – he might go back to the Centre and see if anything else has come in whilst he'd been away. He drained the last of the beer from the can and tried to relax, despite his frustration and anxiety.

The public address system suddenly burst into life. "This is the rig commander. The six crew members who are awaiting transport to the mainland must be ready to depart in thirty minutes. The storm has eased sufficiently to allow the helicopter pilot to take off. Flying conditions are rough but he is managing to navigate through the bad weather. He is bringing the relief crew."

Mark looked at his watch. Dammit, I must have dozed off for an hour at least, he muttered. Quickly gathering his personal belongings, he stuffed them into a duffel bag and rushed out to the radio room. "Hi Steve, I still need to make that personal call now that it looks like communications have been restored."

"Sorry matey, but there's still interference on the airwaves, and all channels have to remain open for the chopper. Think yourself lucky it's on its way, and hope that he'll be able to take off again. You can make that call from base after you've arrived there."

"So you're not open to bribes then," Mark said, trying to curb his frustration with a touch of humour. He knew full well that safety regulations overrode the personal needs of individuals.

"I don't think you could afford my fee," Steve replied with a smile. "Have a safe trip and see you next time. You'd better make your way to the landing pad, as the chopper is due in five minutes. The pilot won't want to hang about in case the storm worsens again."

Mark grunted a response and made his way to the pad. It's still blowing a gale, he thought; I wouldn't want to be the pilot trying to descend onto the rig in wind like this, especially as the light's starting to fade. He watched as the helicopter bobbed and weaved a few times before landing safely. With the rotor still turning, six men rapidly exited the craft and he and five others were quickly ushered onboard.

"Strap yourselves in," the pilot instructed. "I'm taking off right now. If you're going to be airsick with the buffeting, please use the paper bags beneath your seat and don't vomit on the floor like one of the incoming crew members did."

Despite his keenness to be reunited with his family again, Mark was not looking forward to being tossed about inside a small aircraft that probably shouldn't have been flying in such poor weather anyway. If they crash landed in the boiling sea, they wouldn't stand much of a chance of rescue. He wondered if it would have been better to stay on the rig until the storm had passed. Too late now. The pilot pushed the throttle forward, eased back the stick, and the chopper started to ascend, the spinning rotor only marginally missing the drilling derrick.

Mark made an effort to avoid regurgitating his last meal, despite the violent swaying that occurred when the wind caught what seemed to be such a small and fragile sanctuary. "It'll take an estimated thirty minutes to reach my base at Humberside Airport," the pilot announced. "From there the company has provided a minibus to take you to your home towns, or the railway station if outside the local area."

This temporarily distracted Mark from his physical discomfort. The first thing I must do, assuming we arrive at the airport in one piece, is to phone Margaret. Then, if the transport is going as far south as Torcaster, I can walk to my house from there assuming I can't find a taxi. It might be close to midnight, but at least I'll be home. I really don't want to have to go through all this again.

It was now dark outside but, after what seemed to be a much longer time than the pilot estimated, the welcome lights of Humberside Airport came into view. After a practise run to gauge the strength of the cross wind, the pilot attempted a landing. However, the helicopter came down on one skid, with the rotor blades only inches from the ground. It balanced precariously for a few moments, as if deciding for itself whether or not to topple over. Maybe even machines can sometimes be benevolent toward their owners as, with a jolt, both skids then settled onto the tarmac.

The relieved passengers could not resist a spontaneous cheer to be down safe and sound, and it was warm handshakes for the pilot as they alighted. Mark's first priority was to find the nearest phone box to make that call home, but he would have to be quick if he wasn't to miss the minibus.

An airport official pointed him in the right direction. Mark immediately pushed coins into the slot and dialled the number. It rang. He waited. No answer. What could be stopping Margaret answering? Had he made an error with the dialling? He tried again. Still no response. The transport would leave without him if he didn't put the phone down now and dash off to the departure point.

"How long before we reach Torcaster?" he asked the driver, breathless after his exertion. "I'm anxious to get home."

"And so is everyone else who's been starved of female company these last three weeks or more," the driver answered, his face displaying a knowing smirk. "But to answer your question, about an hour."

"But it's less than ten miles, how come it'll take so long?"

"It's not just you I'm taking home, matey. Each of the lads lives in a different town. Torcaster is my last drop off point."

Mark had no alternative but to sit and wait, frequently looking at his watch. After the other passengers had been dropped off, each shouting a cheerful 'good bye' to those who remained, at last the bus arrived in Torcaster. "Can you perhaps take me a bit further? I live just a mile out of town," he asked.

"Sorry mate, my instructions are to leave passengers at the main centres where they can make their own arrangements. I do have a home of my own to get back to, you know."

There was no point in arguing, but he did wonder later if a generous tip might have helped. The town centre was dead: no busses, no taxies, not even any private motorists. Fortunately, the storm was not as severe inland as it was over the sea, but some rain was still falling. Pulling the hood of his jacket over his head and slinging his duffel bag over his shoulder, Mark set off to walk the last leg of the journey.

He looked at his watch again. It would be midnight by the time he reached his house, and Margaret would not be expecting a caller at this ungodly hour. Should he have stayed overnight at the airport and waited until morning before phoning again? If there'd been no public transport, he could always have taken a taxi home.

After half a mile the street lights came to and end. Apart from occasional glimpses of moonlight through breaks in the cloud, and distant house lights from a few night owls, it was pitch black. But he had trodden this path many times before and was familiar with every yard. At last his own home came into view. He had been fortunate to find a detached residence that was affordable, but it was an older house that needed renovations. Being good at practical work, he had been able to do much of it himself.

He was not surprised to see there were no lights on, as his wife and young son would be tucked up in bed and asleep. Mark took out his door key but, before inserting it into the lock, he still wondered how he could avoid giving Margaret a shock at his unexpected appearance at this hour. Should he just knock to arouse her first? If she opened an upstairs window to see who it was, he could reassure her and then go right in. Yes, that's what he would do.

He knocked, not too loudly. Nothing happened. He knocked harder. Still no appearance by his wife. That's surprising, he thought, but maybe she couldn't hear the noise very well from the bedroom. No alternative now but to go inside. He took hold of the door handle and slid his key into the lock but, before he turned it, the door pushed open.

* * *

A myriad of thoughts flashed through Mark's mind. Something's wrong, he could feel it. It was not like Margaret to forget to lock up properly at night. He rushed upstairs and entered the bedroom. His wife was not there. Then into Charlie's room. Empty.

'I must not panic; I must not panic,' he forced himself to say out loud. 'I must get a grip on myself.' A voice inside his head was trying to tell him something. 'Remember the training for emergencies you received before you were allowed onto the oil rig,' it said. 'Panic leads to disaster. Stay calm and think.' Mark obeyed and sat down on the bedroom chair.

Firstly, have a look to see if Margaret has packed some clothes for herself and Charlie. She may have gone to visit someone and simply forgot to lock the front door. It could even have been an emergency like a sick relative, and she'd had to leave in a hurry. Yes, that's a likely explanation. He had a look around the room. No, all the suit cases are there on top of the wardrobe, and I can't see any obvious signs of missing clothes.

Maybe she didn't have time to pack, he thought, or felt she wouldn't need to as she would only be gone a short time. If that's the case, there may be a message on the telephone answer machine, or even a written note left for him in case he came back when she was out. In his haste to look upstairs, he had not yet been in the other rooms. He walked down the stairs rather more slowly than he had ascended, opened the lounge door and switched on the light.

He was not prepared for what he saw, and couldn't suppress shouting out: 'Oh no!' Although the storm was only raging outside, it looked as if it had also caused devastation inside. Chairs were overturned; the bookcase had been knocked over and its contents strewn across the floor. Shards of vases and crockery were everywhere, as was some cutlery and the remains of a meal.

Again Mark tried to control the panic that was starting to envelop him. Take a few deep breaths, his instructor had told him. Feeling only slightly calmer, he looked around more carefully to see if there were any clues to explain what had happened. Ah, there are some splashes of blood on the wall there, but I don't see any bloodstained weapons on the floor. Perhaps someone was injured by flying crockery. Better phone the police before doing anything else; hopefully they'll be able to discover something. He dialled the emergency services. Good, they'll come immediately, but I mustn't touch anything else until they arrive.

He left the lounge and sat on the stairs. What has happened to my darling wife and child? He asked himself. I should never have taken the job on the rig and left them unprotected. It's all my fault. With nothing to do now but wait, the emotion he had been suppressing up to this moment could be contained no longer and the tears started to run down his cheeks.

The noise of a vehicle outside, and a flashing blue light glinting through the glass panel of the front door caused him to make and effort to regain some composure. "I'm glad you came so quickly," he said as two officers in plain clothes stepped into the hallway.

"Good evening Mr Keeley, I'm Detective Sergeant George Goffin. After what you'd described on the telephone I asked the duty CSI Jane Nesbit, to join me." Seeing Mark's puzzled look he said, "Sorry sir, that stands for Crime Scene Investigator. Jane nodded in Mark's direction, and put down her bag of equipment. "Can we start by looking at the room you say was ransacked?"

Mark led them to the door of the lounge. The officers looked into the room but didn't immediately enter. "Did you touch anything when you first saw this?" the sergeant asked.

"I will have touched the door, and of course the telephone," Mark replied, trying to replay in his mind his search of the building barely an hour previously. "I walked around looking at the mayhem, but something inside me warned against deliberately handling anything else. What I did see were blood stains on the wall over there."

"Good, that may make our job easier. Jane, will you please go in first to take photographs and then dust for fingerprints. Whilst you do that I'll sit with the gentleman in another room and take a statement. Come and find us when you've finished." The two men made their way into the kitchen, leaving the CSI to do her job.

"Would you like me to make a cup of tea for us all, before we start?" Mark asked as they sat down at the kitchen table."

"Very kind of you to ask, Sir, but let's leave that until later as we shall need to check the rest of your house when we've finished with the lounge. There may be some clues you may have overlooked. Let's start with the timing. When did you last speak with your wife?"

"I've been working on an oil rig for three weeks, and private calls using the rig's radio equipment were limited. I did manage to talk to her three days ago to say I hoped to be coming home tonight. I requested a call to her again a couple of hours before the helicopter came, but the storm made it impossible to transmit any message."

"When you spoke with her earlier, did she give you any indication there was a problem, or that she was worried about anything?"

"No, it was a normal conversation where we were both looking forward to being together again."

The sergeant paused from writing his notes. "Did you try to telephone her once you arrived back at the airport?"

"Yes, and that's when I started to feel worried," Mark replied. "It must have been about 10pm when I tried to phone from Humberside Airport, but there was no reply. I know she sometimes does go to bed at that time, but she would've stayed up knowing I was expected home that night."

"I see. So what time did you arrive back here at the house?"

"About midnight. I wasn't surprised the house was dark at that hour, but it was obvious that something was wrong when I found that the front door wasn't locked."

"I can understand how worried you would've been," Goffin said. "Your call to the station was timed at 12:14am, so you lost no time in contacting us. All we can say so far is that your wife and son disappeared within the last three days, but I'm sure we can narrow this down."

"I think we can already," said Mark. There are letters waiting for me on the hall table. Margaret will have left them there for me whilst I was away. Let me go and look at the post mark dates to see how long they've been there. Yes, here's one here with a first class stamp and it's dated the day before yesterday."

"That's helpful," the sergeant commented. "It must have been delivered yesterday morning, so that means your wife was at home for at least the first part of the day. Before I go off duty later this morning, I shall organise a door-to-door enquiry with your neighbours to see if they noticed anything suspicious, and to ask when they last saw your family."

"Good idea," said Mark. "But I'm out of my mind with worry; I should never have gone away and left them on their own." He made an effort to suppress the emotion that started to well up again.

Goffin put his hand on Mark's shoulder. "I'd feel exactly the same if it were my family, but we'll do all we can to find your wife and child. What I need now is a full description of your wife, so I can start a missing person's search."

"There's a photograph of Margaret with Charlie in the lounge. I took it when we were on holiday last summer. You can borrow it if you wish, but please take good care of it."

"Thank you, sir, that'll be very helpful. Can you let me have a verbal description of her?"

"She's about five foot six inches, with blond hair and green eyes. It's those eyes that I found so attractive when we first met. She's aged twenty-eight, two years younger than me. We've been married for five years now, and little Charlie came along a year later. We'd planned to try for another child once we could afford it, which is one of the reasons I took the job on that damned oil rig. But it's all gone wrong now."

Let's see what our CSI has found, and then maybe we can have that tea you offered earlier," the sergeant said, deciding it would be best to pause the questioning for a while to give Mark time to regain his composure. He put his head round the door to the lounge. "How are you doing, Jane? Do you need more time?"

"Just about finished Gee Gee," she said, using the nickname she had for George Goffin. "Will be with you in a minute or two."

The sergeant returned to the kitchen. "If you want to put the kettle on Jane will join us soon, and we can review what we know."

* * *

Glad for the chance to stand up and do something useful, Mark collected the mugs and then looked in the biscuit tin. It had been many hours since he had last eaten and his stomach was now protesting. "The milk in the fridge is still fresh," he called out to the sergeant. "That confirms Margaret was here until very recently."

"Right, Jane, what can you tell us?" Goffin asked when they were all sitting at the kitchen table, a plate of biscuits and steaming mugs of tea in front of them.

"I've photographed everything and dusted for fingerprints. I used the hand vacuum I brought with me to collect some hairs, and also swabbed the blood stain on the wall." Turning to Mark she said, "Do you know your own blood group, and that of your wife?"

"I do, because I had to undergo a thorough medical before being allowed onto the rig. Margaret had her blood type done when she was pregnant. Mine is A-positive, and hers is B-negative. I even know Charlie's, because it was thought he might be anaemic when he was born. He is AB-positive."

"Excellent," the CSI said. "Are you able to give me some samples of her hair, perhaps from a comb or brush? Maybe also from your little son if he has his own brush. I shall also need to take your fingerprints. If you can find something that might have your wife's prints on, please don't touch it but just let me know."

Mark got up from his chair. "Okay," he replied. "I'll go upstairs and see what I can find." A few moments later he shouted down to Jane: "I can see two hair brushes and a glass bottle of eau do cologne. You can come up here and take them as samples."

"Excellent," she said, once the items were safely inside a plastic bag. "I'll also take a few hairs from you, so that I can compare what I've vacuumed with those from all three of you. That's about it from me until I have the results of the forensic tests. You can go into the lounge now and proceed with your investigation, Gee Gee."

Goffin put down his tea cup. "Okay Jane, thanks. You go and pack up your equipment whilst I ask Mr Keeley just a few more questions." He turned to face Mark. "How long have you lived in this house?"

"We moved here two years ago and bought it at a good price because it was run down and needed a lot doing to it. I've spent all my spare time and money on the renovations."

"I can see you're very good at do-it-yourself; it certainly saves a lot of money if you have the know-how. How well do you know your neighbours?"

Mark thought for a moment. "Not very well. These houses are away from the urban area and are spaced out with some land between them. There's a nice retired couple in the house just in front of ours, and we always say 'hello' when we see them. The man in the house behind walks his dog along the lane each day; he looks in our direction and nods but doesn't speak to us. I'm not sure if there's anyone else living there with him."

The sergeant made a note in his book. "Just one final question, as I know this is distressing for you, but do you know of anyone who might hold a grudge against you. Or even someone who is jealous that you married the woman they fancied?"

"I do understand you have to ask things like this. Margaret is an attractive woman, and I wasn't the only boyfriend she had. There may have been someone who resented being passed over, and who's still looking for a way to get back at us."

"Do you have any names?"

"Sorry, no. You would have to ask Margaret that, but of course she's not here."

"Of course, sir. I think we can leave it at that for the present. I better start my own investigation now. You can join me if you like, so I can check things with you if I need to."

The two men went into the lounge. Mark's heart started to race again the moment he saw the devastation. "Let's try and summarise what we know," Goffin said in a calm voice. "Was there any sign of forced entry to the front door when you arrived home?"

"No, only that it wasn't locked when I entered."

"And you didn't see any signs of damage or disruption until you entered the lounge?"

"Well I certainly didn't notice anything, but then I wasn't looking in detail, and all the lights were off at the time."

"I understand," the sergeant commented quietly. "I'm sure you'll agree it's likely your wife freely let someone into the house, and that the trouble only began when they were here in the lounge."

"Yes, it does look like that. But then there must have been a fight to cause all this mess."

"Certainly; your wife must have defended herself well and probably thrown vases and anything else she could lay her hands on at whomever it was who was with her."

"It's upsetting to think of what went on here," Mark said in a soft voice. "And there's that blood on the wall, so Margaret might be badly injured."

"I wouldn't say that, sir." Goffin replied. "It's only a smudge and there's none on the carpet. Also, it might well be from the attacker who was hit by broken crockery."

"Let's hope so, but where have she and Charlie been taken?"

"We'll do our very best to find out, and bring them back to you. I know how you must feel, but let me just have a final look round and then I'll help you clear up in here and put the furniture back where it belongs."

"That's very kind of you," said Mark. "But the activity will help me feel I'm doing something useful. I'm sure you and your colleague want to get back to the station to complete your reports."

"If you're confident about that, sir," the Sergeant said. "It's now three o'clock in the morning, and it'll be useful for me to organise the house-to-house enquiries as well as make sure the samples get to the forensic lab for analysis. Are you going to stay in the house on your own, or go to a friend or relative for company? I need to know where you can be contacted."

"I've no friends or relatives around here," Mark said. You can just use my home telephone. If I do go out, I'll contact the station and leave a message for you."

"Very well, Mr Keeley. I know it's easy to say but not easy to do, but try and stay calm and be assured we shall all be doing our very best to find your wife and son."

The two officers departed, and left Mark to try and come to terms with the traumatic events of the last twenty-four hours. He began to sort out the mess in the lounge but fatigue started to take over so he made his way upstairs and flopped down on the bed.

Sleep came quickly, at least for two hours, but then his level of consciousness rose to that state where dreams occur. He was riding in an aircraft. It was falling, falling, falling. It crashed but he just walked away from the wreckage unscathed. He was lost, wandering in a strange land. People passed by and he called out to them: 'Please help me.' But they just walked on as if they could not see or hear him. He was now alone, struggling to make headway but his feet were encased in stone. It would have been easy to give up but he persisted. Darkness then descended as deep sleep again enveloped him.

Now the fantasies returned. He was surrounded by dogs, dogs of all sizes and colours, all looking at him. A large black one approached and stood on its hind legs so that its face was on a level with his. It spoke: 'What are you doing here? You don't belong in this place.' 'Sorry,' he replied. 'I'm lost. Can you tell me how to get back to my own land?' 'You will have to work that out for yourself,' said the dog. 'There are clues to help you if you seek them. 'But I don't know where to start,' Mark said. 'You must look at all the possibilities,' his canine companion persisted. 'One of them will point the way.' The image faded and the veil came down once more.

* * *

Mark looked at the bedside clock. It was eight o'clock. He was surprised he had managed to sleep at all, but his four hours of slumber had revived him. The remnants of his dreams came back to him. How stupid these fantasies are, he thought, but I remember being lost and begging for help. Now what was it the dog said? Something like there are clues and many possibilities, and one of them will point the way. Now what could that mean?

Putting it out of his mind, at least for now, he went to the bathroom and splashed cold water on his face before going downstairs. Entering the lounge and seeing the mess that remained immediately rekindled his anxiety and sadness. Realising that he must make a big effort to think clearly and avoid panic, he finished tidying up the lounge before looking for something to eat. Once he had swept up the broken crockery, he fetched a damp cloth and wiped the blood stains from the wall. I do hope and pray these don't belong to Margaret or Charlie, he said to himself, swallowing hard to stave off the tears that were not far away.

He felt a little calmer after a good breakfast, prepared from the plentiful supply of food in the kitchen. Having all this in the larder just confirms that Margaret was not intending to be away at this time, he thought.

The door bell rang. "Good morning Mr Keeley," a uniformed police officer said. "I'm Constable Fred Wilkinson, and am here to conduct house-to-house enquiries. But I'd just like to ask you about your neighbours before I start."

Mark was reassured to have the presence of a law enforcement officer with him again, and know that action was being taken to try and solve his case. "Do come in, officer. How can I help you? I did tell Sergeant Goffin everything I knew about them last night."

"Yes sir, I've read the report he left before he went off duty at seven this morning. He'll be on dayshift from Monday and will remain the chief investigating officer for this case."

"Do you mean that no effort will be taken this weekend to find my wife and son?" Mark said, making an effort to control his anger. "It's not right; every hour of every day is crucial. They could be in mortal danger this very minute!"

"No, no. That's not the situation, sir I can assure you," Wilkinson replied quickly. "A description of your missing family and the photograph has already been circulated to all forces in the county and those adjoining it. Also to the ports along the east coast. The forensic laboratory is right now analysing the samples that were taken last night. As soon as there's something to report, the duty detective inspector will contact you."

"Of course you're right, and I'm very sorry I nearly lost my temper just now," Mark said, feeling ashamed of himself that his anxiety had taken over.

"Not at all, Mr Keeley," the constable replied calmly. "If it were my wife and son that were missing I'd be just as distraught as you are. Be confident that no effort is being spared to find your loved ones, and all avenues are being explored. Now, before I go round and visit your neighbours, could you just reiterate what you told the officer last night. Maybe you've thought of some additional details that might be useful."

"There's really not much I can tell you. As I mentioned to the sergeant, the retired couple who live in the first house on the lane seem very pleasant. We always exchange greetings and occasional small talk such as the weather. When I drive past their house I often see the man working in the front garden."

"Do you know their names?"

"I'm ashamed to say that I don't," Mark replied, realising too late that he hadn't made much of an effort to be sociable with those around him. "In the two years we've been here I've spent all my time when not out at work in renovating the house. Margaret helps me when she can. We've just really kept ourselves to ourselves most of the time."

The constable made notes in his book. "I'll go round and see them first. Now you mentioned something to my colleague about the man in the house behind you."

"Yes. You'll have seen that the houses here are well spaced apart, and some properties have enough land to grow crops or keep small animals. All I know about the third house is that a man lives there. There may be someone else, but I've only seen him."

"Can you give me a description?"

"Only that he looks to be about middle age and of average height. He always wears a coat and an old type trilby hat, and he takes his dog for a walk every day. When we're in our front garden he looks in our direction, but then just nods and walks on if we try to say anything to him. I suppose this is unsociable, but we don't take offence as we are all different and he doesn't cause any trouble."

"Thank you sir; I'll also call on him. And what about the houses beyond?"

"Afraid I can't tell you anything. I've driven along the road just to see what's there. As I mentioned, some make good use of their spacious land, but I don't know any of the occupants except to see them drive past our place."

"Very good, Mr Keeley," the officer said closing his note book. "I'll go and start my door to door enquiries now. Once again, please be assured that everything is being done to find your wife and child as quickly as possible. You'll be kept in formed of any developments." With that he departed, leaving Mark on his own to try and come to terms with the events of the last twenty-four hours.

I can't believe that this time yesterday I was all packed up and ready to be taken off the rig, he said to himself. But then the helicopter had to be delayed due to that damned storm. If only I could've made that call to Margaret, as I'm sure she would still have been in the house then. If everything had gone to plan I'd have been home early afternoon. There's nothing more I can do except wait for the police to do their job, I suppose. Might as well go and make myself some coffee.

Ten minutes later, settled in a chair armed with a steaming mug of beverage, his mind went back to the dream. Usually I don't remember them, he thought, but there was something different about this one. The image of the talking dog standing on its hind legs and telling me there are clues I must search for, and that one of them will point the way. But that was because I was lost and needed to find my way back home. I wonder if that could have implied there were clues to help me find out where Margaret and Charlie are. Let me think carefully.

The ringing of the telephone jolted Mark out of his deliberations. "Mr Keeley?"

"Yes, that's me."

"This is Detective Inspector Tooley from Torcaster police headquarters."

"Have you found my wife and son?" Mark blurted out, his anxiety instantly rekindled.

"Not yet sir," the inspector replied calmly. "But we are investigating every possibility. In the meantime, I do have some news I thought you would want to hear. The forensics team have managed to check the blood stain that was on your wall, and the group does not match either of your missing family members."

"Well, that's good to know. Margaret must have managed to injure the attacker, probably by throwing crockery at him."

"I agree," the D.I. said. "But of course we don't yet know if the intruder was a he or a she. By the way, I didn't see any reference in Sergeant Goffin's report about you owning a dog."

"That's because we don't," Mark replied. "What makes you say this?"

"It's another result from forensics. Some of the hairs the investigator vacuumed up were from a dog. Have you been visited by anyone who owns one of these animals?"

"Not that I know of. Certainly none of our friends or relatives has one."

"Okay Mr Heeley, that's something for us to consider. Has P.C. Wilkinson been to see you this morning?"

"Yes, he left a short while ago to conduct his house to house enquiries."

"Good," Tooley said. "That's all for now but someone will be in touch the moment we have any news or questions. Goodbye."

Mark returned to his chair and picked up his coffee cup. At least the police are moving quickly, he thought. But Margaret and Charlie remain in danger with every minute that passes. He drained the last of his drink and tried to think through the latest developments. Well done Margaret for managing to injure the intruder, but what about the dog hairs? Why do dogs keep entering the picture? First I'm advised in my dream by a dog, and then the Inspector says dog hairs were found in the lounge. We don't know anyone with a dog . . . or maybe we do. Our neighbour in the house behind walks a dog every day. I think it's about time I paid him a visit.

* * *

Without any thought that it might be risky to visit an individual he didn't know alone, Mark walked down his drive, turned left into the lane, and then left again toward his neighbour's house. The unpaved path up to the front door was muddy due to the previous night's storm, and footprints of different sizes were clearly visible.

He knocked on the door. There were sounds of movement from inside the house, but the door remained closed. He knocked again. Now he could hear a dog barking, but still nobody came. Mark was determined to stay as long as necessary, and repeated his hammering. His patience was rewarded when the door finally opened a few inches but remained secured by a chain. "Good morning, I live in the house in front of you," he said in as friendly a tone as he could muster. "Can I perhaps have a word with you please?"

He could just make out one eye and half the face of a man whom he judged to be approaching middle age. "What do you want?" the occupant said in a voice verging on the hostile. "I don't like opening the door to strangers."

"Sorry to be troubling you, but I see you walk past my house with your dog most days," Mark said, making an effort to remain friendly. "My wife and child went missing yesterday when I was away, and I just wondered if you might have seen or heard anything that might be useful to the police."

"No, I don't know anything. Now will you go away and leave me in peace."

Mark started to think he was wasting his time and perhaps should leave rather than try and be more forceful, but then he heard the dog barking. The man left the door and went to quieten it, and he used the opportunity to peer through the gap into the hall. It looked dirty and untidy, and so did the inhabitant from the bit he could see of him. His neighbour was shouting at the dog, but then there was another sound. It was only faint, but he was sure it was of a child crying.

His level of adrenalin rose sharply. I'm going in whether it's legal or not, he said to himself. Pushing his shoulder against the door he broke the fitting of the security chain and ran into the hall. Yes, there was definitely a child crying, and it sounded familiar. The man turned and shouted at him to get out, but Mark continued until he was face to face with him. "Where are my wife and child?" he demanded.

"I don't know what you're talking about. You're trespassing in my house. Just get out now, or you'll be in trouble."

Mark could see there was a door next to where they were standing, and it was secured with a bolt on the outside. If the layout of the house was similar to mine, he thought, it will lead down into the cellar. The crying sounded to be coming from down there. He moved his hand to slide open the bolt but, before he could do so, his fingers were struck a hefty blow with a wooden object. Uttering an involuntary yelp, he quickly pulled his hand away. It felt like something might be broken.

"I told you to get out but you didn't listen," the man said, raising a baseball bat in the air. Now you're going to pay the price for it. Mark lifted his other hand to try and protect himself as the weapon descended, but his attacker suddenly crumpled and fell to the floor. Constable Wilkinson slid his truncheon back into its pocket and snapped a pair of handcuffs on the dazed individual before he could recover enough to stand up.

"You came at the right moment," Mark said breathlessly, trying to regain his composure. "Thank you so much; you probably saved my life."

"All part of the job," the constable replied calmly. "I'd finished interviewing Mr and Mrs Simms and was making my way to this house when I saw the door open and heard the commotion. I came right in and did what had to be done."

"I'm certainly glad you did, but let's now see what's behind this door." Mark slid open the bolt with his good hand, pulled back on the handle and peered inside. It was dark and at first he could see nothing. The light switch was on the outside and he flipped it on. Yes, it was a cellar, and two figures were standing at the bottom of the steps, rubbing their eyes and looking up at him."

"Daddy!" Charlie shouted and started to climb up the stairs. Margaret followed him, her eyes now becoming used to the light again. Throwing their arms around each other, the tears of relief flowed.

"Are you both alright?" Mark asked, once the emotion had eased enough to make normal conversation possible.

"We're rather cold and hungry, but otherwise not injured," Margaret replied, not wishing to release her tight hold on her husband."

PC Wilkinson had maintained a respectful silence whilst the reunion took place, concentrating on guarding his prisoner, but he now needed to ask a question. "Madam, do you know this man?"

"I didn't recognise him until last night. His name is Gordon Littlewood. Many years ago, before I met my husband, we went out on a couple of dates. But, when Mark appeared on the scene, I knew he was the one and stopped seeing Littlewood."

"Have you had any contact with him since then?" the Constable asked.

"Not until yesterday afternoon when he was out with his dog, and knocked on the door. When I opened it he told me his name, and said he realised who I was when he looked across at us. Because he always wore a hat and coat, and never spoke or came near, I had no idea it was him."

"So did you invite him into the house?"

"Not intentionally, but he let his dog off the lead and it bolted inside. Charlie was frightened and I rushed in after him. Fortunately the dog just wanted to play but, when I looked round, Littlewood was there right behind me."

"That must have been worrying for you, darling," Mark commented.

"Not at first," Margaret continued. "But then he said he still wanted to have an affair with me. He had seen that Mark was not at home, so it would be a good time to do this. Of course I refused, saying I was happily married, and that he must go now."

Wilkinson had been taking notes whilst making sure his prisoner remained on the floor. "Can you tell us how you came to be in the cellar, if it's not too traumatic?" he asked.

"When I told him to leave he tried to grab hold of me, but I managed to push him off. He kept trying to catch me, but I threw everything at him

I could grab hold of. He then picked up Charlie and rushed out of the house with him. Of course I followed, and we arrived here at his place. He had already put Charlie on the cellar steps and, when I went in to get him, he slammed the door and locked it."

"You were very brave," Mark said, kissing Margaret on he cheek. "I'm so glad neither of you were injured."

"Littlewood shouted through the door that there would be no food or drink for either of us until I gave in to his wishes," she continued. "Also, the light would remain off. I expected this would last for days. I wasn't concerned about myself, but didn't want Charlie to suffer. Spending last night down there was terrible, and I was starting to wonder what to do next. It was a miracle you came when you did."

"Actually, it wasn't so much a miracle as a dream," Mark said. "Plus a contribution from forensic science," he added.

"Well, it looks like we have enough detail to put Mr Littlewood away for several years," the officer said. "Can I please ask you to see if there's a telephone in this house. I don't want to let go of the prisoner so, if you find it, can you put a call through to the station and tell them we need a squad car and two officers to take him away."

Mark and Margaret took Charlie to search for the telephone. Constable Wilkinson started to return his note book and pencil to his tunic pocket, when Littlewood suddenly jumped up, kneed him in the groin and started to run down the hall. He didn't see his dog lying asleep on the floor. Losing his footing, he tumbled head first, unable to protect himself with his shackled hands.

"That's very careless of me," the officer said as Mark and family rushed back to see what the commotion was. "He wouldn't have gone far with his handcuffs on, but I shouldn't have taken my eyes off him for a second."

"Once again a dog has played a part," Mark commented. "But are you alright, officer?"

"I've suffered worse doing this job, thank you, but did you manage to contact the station?"

"Yes, the squad car will be here shortly."

"Good. Let's take our prisoner outside," Wilkinson said, dragging Littlewood to his feet.

"What about his dog?" Margaret asked as they were leaving.

It was Littlewood himself who answered: "I don't care what happens to it; just have it put down. It's been nothing but trouble."

"Then I'll contact the dog pound to have the animal taken away," the Constable declared.

"But Littlewood did say he didn't care what happened to it, so perhaps we can adopt it," Mark said. He looked toward his wife, and she nodded. "After all, if it hadn't been for dogs, you might still be a prisoner in that cellar."

The Water of Life

"'Morning' Ken, do come in," George said as he welcomed his friend who had arrived for another of their Friday get-togethers to chat and put the world to rights. "Go into the lounge whilst I finish making the coffee."

"It's not a bad day out there," Ken reported, hanging up his coat. "Maybe we should go for a walk and then call at the pub on the way back for a lunchtime pint."

"A good idea," his friend replied, placing the filled cups on the side table. "But there's something I want to chat to you about first."

"Right, I'm listening; not another of your wild ideas I hope."

George gave a mock frown. There was always a bit of friendly jousting between them and he knew this was only meant as a joke, but this time it might be true. "Actually, in this case you may have a point, but I've been given something and I'm not sure what to do with it."

"Hmm, sounds intriguing; I'm all ears," said Ken, taking a sip of his coffee and munching at a chocolate biscuit.

"Well, you know I've long been intrigued by that Hindu temple in Waterborough. The other day an Indian neighbour offered to take me there to see inside the building, and I was pleased to accept his invitation."

"Sounds interesting; I'd like to have a look in there myself. But do go on."

"When you go in, you first have to take your shoes off, and then you walk past the main congregational hall and through to a stage at the back. There, under the lights, are life-sized colourful statues of all the different Hindu gods. It's quite an impressive sight."

"I'm now even keener to go and see them for myself," Ken remarked.

"As we were looking at these figures, the priest came out and spoke with us," continued George. "I say 'us,' but his English was poor and my friend had to translate for me. Seeing a donations box next to the stage, I made a contribution. The priest seemed very pleased with this, and he disappeared into his office, asking us to wait a moment."

"This is all very intriguing," said Ken. "What happened then?"

"He came back with a traditional cake in a packet, and a tiny bottle of water,"

George said, pleased that his friend now appeared to be genuinely interested. "My neighbour explained later that it was customary to take some food into the temple, and to be given something in return by the priest."

"And did you eat and drink these?"

"I ate the cake, but I still have the water, and it's what I want to discuss," replied George, producing a small brown bottle containing 25 millilitres of liquid. "It states on the label that it's sanctified water offered to the shrine of Akshar Deri in India."

"So what are you meant to do with it? It's obviously too small to be a thirst quencher."

"You drink it, and the priest said it will enable you to live for ever!"

"Ah well, I enjoyed your story whilst it lasted," Ken said with a laugh. "I've finished my coffee, so we can go on that walk now if you're ready."

"Actually I'm being serious," George replied, the expression on his face indicating he was a little disappointed by his friend's reaction.

Realising he may have been a bit hasty, Ken said, "Sorry George, but you don't really believe that claim do you?"

"What is there to lose if I drink it?" George asked. "It surely can't do any harm. Shall we have half each and see what happens?"

Ken shook his head. "No thanks, but you go ahead if you really want to. I don't know how you'll be able to tell if it works, at least not until you surpass the age of 120, which I believe the boffins say is about our maximum life span."

"I'm sure I can be patient," said George, as he unscrewed the bottle cap. He then poured the liquid into his mouth, swilled it around a few times, and swallowed it.

"What does it taste like?" his friend asked.

"It doesn't taste of anything, just plain water with no sparkle."

"Do you want to wait a few minutes before we set off, in case you start to feel weird or grow an extra head or something?" Ken asked, unable to resist any opportunity to inject some humour into the situation.

George ignored the witticism, and only hesitated for a moment before replying, "No, thanks, I don't see any problem. We can go now."

"Being able to live for ever does raise some interesting questions," Ken said, as they walked along in the direction of the *World's End* pub. "What would folk do with their lives if they knew they would never die?

"Well, there are people mentioned in the Bible who lived an awfully long time," commented

George. "Noah is said to have reached the age of 950, and even became a father when he was 500 years old."

"Hmm, that raises some interesting possibilities," Ken replied cheekily. "But knowing that you'd be in the same job for all eternity might not be a very exciting existence, and no pension provider could afford to let you retire in your sixties or seventies."

"I agree it's something to consider," George conceded, "But maybe one could change jobs and learn new skills every fifty years or so, just to keep from becoming bored. Just think of the challenges: you could make a new start to your life every century."

"And what about producing children?" Ken asked. "If very few people died, and most of the rest kept breeding, this Earth would soon be so crowded that folk would start dropping off the edge!"

"Alright clever Dick, I agree these issues would make it difficult if nearly everyone lived for ever," George said, torn between trying to be serious and treating the whole thing as a joke. "But if we did continue having babies, it might be difficult to keep track of your infinitesimal levels of grandchildren to ensure that each one receives a birthday card!"

"Glad you can also see the funny side," said Ken, as the *World's End* came into sight. "But I'm still wondering why you actually had to drink the water. Has it had any effect on you so far?"

"Now that you mention it, I am feeling a bit queasy. Maybe a pint of the amber nectar would help to settle my stomach."

"Or it might have the opposite effect," Ken quickly commented. "Perhaps we should just give the pub a miss this time and head off back to your house before you feel any worse."

"I guess you're right," conceded George. "It *is* getting worse, and I think I'm going to be sick."

No sooner had they turned around than Ken saw his friend starting to retch, and then collapse onto the pavement. "I'm going to call for an ambulance," he said, taking out his mobile phone, and ignoring George's attempt to protest.

The emergency vehicle arrived within minutes, and the paramedics immediately stretchered their patient into the vehicle.

"His temperature's up, and it looks like he's starting a fever," one of the medical team said after his initial examination. "He may have acute food poisoning. Has your friend been eating any unusual or stale foods today?"

"No," Ken responded. "But he did drink some bottled water just over an hour ago. It came from overseas."

"Well that might be the cause then. Some of these foreign bugs can be very severe. We must get him into hospital for tests to see if the microbe can be identified, and then treated. Hopefully it'll respond to the antibiotics."

The ambulance sped away, leaving Ken to think back over their discussion that morning. Rather than bestowing the gift of an everlasting life, George would be fortunate if the sanctified water didn't bring it to a premature end.

Aliens and Religion

From time to time we see articles or even whole books that suggest the Earth was visited by extra-terrestrials many years ago. Among the evidence cited is the fabrication of major buildings such as the Egyptian pyramids and the Mayan temples, with claims that this would not have been possible with the technology available at the time. Is this being unfair to the citizens of these countries who were responsible for the design and construction of those large, impressive edifices, or were they helped?

When there is a lack of hard evidence, we are very good at using our imagination to fill the gaps with conspiratory theories, or speculations of visits by aliens. In fact, the very idea that we are not alone, or are being watched, or have been visited, is a recurring theme popular with writers, film makers, and researchers. An influential book originally published in 1968 by Erich von Däniken, *Chariots of the Gods* (Econ Publishing, Düsseldorf) presented examples and images as evidence to support his conviction that we have been visited.

However, what may be proof to one person is mere speculation to another. As the evidence becomes stronger, and more frequent, we may think we're closing in on unequivocal proof. But, in the case of a visitation from another world, the only real proof would be if an extra terrestrial came down to earth and introduced itself. In the absence of such an event, we've little alternative but to continue adding to what we think is evidence to show this has already occurred.

Having said this, only looking for examples that support a preconceived view is not good research. The 'scientific method' requires that we devote just as much effort toward finding alternative explanations for any proposition. If we don't succeed, then our original idea is strengthened.

The present enquiry is not concerned with citing impressive buildings like the pyramids to support claims that we have been visited by aliens. Instead, it investigates whether or not ancient images of unusual beings could be linked in any way to the dawn of religious beliefs.

Rock art, statues, monuments and stele, some dating back several thousand years, exist in many countries throughout the world. What is even more surprising is that there is often a striking similarity between them. Many of them fall into one of three basic configurations. The first to be considered here are clearly identifiable as hybrids of humans and animals, either a human head on an animal body, or an animal head on a human body.

Perhaps the best known example of an animal sculpture with a human head is the Great Sphinx of Giza, Egypt, which has been dated to about 2,500 BCE. Monuments in Mesopotamia include a winged and crow-footed female figure from the 19th to 18th century BCE. Colossal statues of a bearded man's head on the winged body of a lion or bull are more recent, dating from the ninth century BCE. Centaurs often feature in Greek mythology, having the upper body of a man and the legs of a horse. These were first mentioned in the sixth to fifth centuries BCE.

The ancient Egyptians also had many gods that are depicted as human-like but with an animal's head. These include Anubis (dog), Horus (falcon) and Sobek (crocodile). Statues and pyramid texts featuring such deities date from around 3,000 to 1,500 BCE. Why should such human-animal hybrids have been so popular in ancient cultures? If they really are aliens, then maybe the visitors took animal form to help them be accepted by humans. Alternatively, if they were just products of human imagination, then perhaps people just admired qualities the animals had such as strength or ability to fly. Projecting these onto their gods gave them abilities that ordinary mortals don't possess.

Most examples of the second of category are located in Central America, and comprise human-like figures that are usually seated in a capsule. Their appearance has helped to ferment the notion that these are astronauts piloting spaceships.

The earliest example is the Olmec La Venta Stele 19 from ancient Mexico, a sculpture dating from 900 to 400 BCE. It's usually referred to as 'the feathered serpent' because it depicts the front part of a large snake with what appear to be feathers on its head. The crouched figure beneath it is wearing some device around its head. It has one arm outstretched, holding something resembling a hand bag. With imagination, it could be interpreted as someone controlling a vehicle.

Another sculpture from the same site is also noteworthy. It depicts a gnome-like individual sitting with arms forward in the same position as we would be in when driving a motor vehicle. But it also bears a remarkable resemblance to an image of the Maori god Porangahau from New Zealand, on the opposite side of the globe. Is this just a coincidence, or 'proof' that the same alien creatures visited both countries? Historians speculate that the Polynesian ancestors of the Maoris may also have reached South America. If they'd then migrated to the central regions, they could have imported their legend of the flying god there as well as to Australasia.

An image from Egypt shows the god Hapi underneath a giant flying snake, as with the La Venta Stele, and he appears to be manipulating something. However, although from a more recent era, the most spaceman-like depiction is found back in Central America. It is of the Maya King K'inich Janaab' Pakal (603-683 CE). He is seated inside a capsule-like structure, and appears to have his hands and feet on some controls. Those who believe we have been visited by aliens find this carving strongly supports their argument.

The third and final image category is the most intriguing. These comprise primitive cave drawings of figures that resemble humans but with unusual additions, usually on the head. Most commonly these are spikes all the way round it, sometimes with a dome that resembles a diver's or astronaut's helmet. These have been found in widely separated countries in the world.

Of particular interest are those at Thompson Springs, Utah, in the western half of North America. One image shows humanoid figures with round heads, or globes around their heads, encircled with a mass of spikes. Another depicts beings with triangular bodies and angular heads, with similar adornments. A third contains similar triangular forms but this time the heads sport a pair of horns, some straight but others bent back in an inverted 'U'. These pictures were created by the Ancestral Puebloan Anasazi peoples, and may have been created between 1,200 and 2,000 BCE.

Very similar images are depicted in rock art from the Val Camonica region in Northern Italy, and thousands of these have been discovered on surfaces throughout the valley. One is even labelled 'The Astronauts' due to its likeness to human figures with globes covered with spikes on their heads. This drawing has been dated to about 1,000 BCE, but others in the region may be thousands of years older.

Yet another example is found in Australia, painted by the Aboriginal people that have inhabited this part of the world since about 2,000 BCE, although the date of this particular image is not known. It depicts the head and shoulders of an individual, and once again the head is encircled with spikes, in this case with small knobs at the ends. The face just features two round eyes with a short vertical line between them. If this represents a nose, then the mouth is absent.

In addition to these three main categories, there is a variety of rock art from many parts of the African continent, the earliest dating from around

1,000 BCE. Many are more humanoid than those previously discussed, but some have distortions. These include heads that look like tulip flowers, or have what may be horns, either droopy or upright. It's unclear whether or not they are intending to depict alien beings, or just adornments of their own people. Finally, we shouldn't forget the Hindu gods such as Ganesha with the elephant head, and Matsya who has the tail of a fish.

This far from exhaustive review of ancient artwork indicates that depictions of beings that are not quite human are found throughout much of the world. In some cases there are striking similarities between images originating from widely separated countries. Is it possible to draw any inference from this, especially as many date from a similar era – 1,000 to 2,000 BCE? We shall leave this question for the moment, and consider the origins of some of the world's major religions.

The very first indications that human beings embraced any form of religious belief are probably hidden in the mists of time. This would have been eons before written records were produced, so we can only investigate using archaeological evidence. Did early man believe celestial bodies such as the sun and moon to be objects that needed to be venerated to ensure they didn't suddenly leave them in the dark? Perhaps they thought certain artefacts had special powers, and they too had to idolised. Maybe certain crafty individuals took advantage of this, and claimed they were in contact with some controlling force, thereby achieving priest-like status.

We can only speculate that our distant ancestors may have started to wonder if there was a creator, and what happened to people after they'd died. Indeed, the earliest evidence of such beliefs are burial sites dating back thirty or forty millennia, where it appears that care had been taken to protect the body from scavengers. A statue dating from this period was discovered in Germany. It was given the name 'Lion-man' because it seems to give human characteristics to an animal. It was the forerunner of the many hybrid deities that became popular many years later.

The first structure that could be a communal place of worship was identified from ruins discovered at Gobeklitepe in Turkey. It was constructed in about 10,000 BCE, pre-dating the first Egyptian tombs by several thousand years. Pyramid construction commenced around 2,650 BCE, with the Step Pyramid of Djoser at Saqqara.

The two oldest religions that are still practiced today are Hinduism and Judaism, both of which originated about 2,000 BCE. Hinduism had no single founder, but there is limited evidence that the earliest civilisation in India practiced a religion that was in some ways similar to later Hinduism. Although there are many gods, some being human-animal hybrids as discussed earlier, they are all believed to be manifestations of the same supreme god or divine energy.

A key text for the Hindus is the *Bhagavad-Gita*, which comprises a dialogue between a warrior and the god Lord Krishna. It has been suggested that there are some parallels between this deity and Jesus Christ.

Turning now to Judaism, from which both Christianity and Islam stemmed, as well as the Jewish faith itself, its date of origin is dependent on what is taken as the starting point. The earliest biblical texts, those of the Pentateuch, are believed by many to have been written by the prophet Moses in about 1,440 BCE, but they relate to events that occurred some five hundred or more years earlier.

The earliest mention in the Hebrew Scriptures of a creature with both human and animal characteristics is found in Genesis, with the introduction of the evil, talking serpent in the Garden of Eden. Flying angels, with or without wings, sometimes referred to as cherubim or seraphim, are mentioned in Exodus and other texts.

This brings us back to the prevalence of human-animal hybrid images found in rock art and ancient sculptures in many countries of the world. Could there be any significant link between these and the origin of religious deities? Was the Earth visited some 4,000 years ago by travellers from another planet, leaving memories initially preserved only through oral tradition and some primitive illustrations?

Without wishing to enter the world of fantasy and wild speculation, this apparent coincidence deserves at least some initial discussion to see if can be either supported or just allocated to the genre of science fiction.

If we have indeed been visited by alien beings, what sort of creatures could they have been? Although we can't estimate this simply by looking at life on our own world, we can consider what characteristics the travellers would have had to possess in order to be advanced enough for intergalactic missions. Their development would have to have followed certain basic rules or principles, and investigators have suggested what these might be.

Firstly, inhabitants of another world would need to have adapted to the resources of their own planet in order to obtain food, protect themselves, and reproduce. It's unlikely that any species could advance if their members remain solitary. Thus, there would most likely be communities that collaborated to achieve more than could any solitary individual.

Then there's the matter of mobility. A plant attached to a rock would have difficulty achieving an advanced state, even though its seeds could be spread by wind or water. The advantages of movement are that you can both explore your environment and escape from danger. If you have appendages or wings, you can move quickly on land or through the atmosphere; if you have swimming aids you can travel through a liquid. But if all you can do is crawl on the ground, you are more restricted and also liable to be caught by anything that can move more quickly.

Researchers into the possibilities of alien life tell us that it's a great advantage to have a symmetrical body. This means advanced creatures would probably have a front and back, and a left and right, rather than be round or triangular. Also, having an even number of legs enables faster movement.

Finally, successful beings would need to have sense organs. We humans have our five senses, including seeing and hearing, but animals such as bats make use of echo sounding similar to radar. Others may utilise electrical fields, chemical detection, or the magnetic force of their world to find their way around.

The conclusion that can be drawn from such thinking is that life-forms from other worlds that have developed the intelligence and knowledge to undertake interplanetary travel might not look vastly different from us. If this is indeed the case, could it be that the widespread depiction of semi-humanoid figures in ancient sculptures and cave paintings indicate that our Earth was actually visited by extra-terrestrial beings some three to four thousand years ago? Taking this speculation one stage further, is it just a coincidence that at about the same time our religion evolved to the stage where gods were portrayed in human or hybrid form?

There are many questions and few answers, but maybe food for thought.

The Observer

I was born forty-million years ago, and have been observing the world ever since. Although I can see, I'm unable to move of my own volition. One day when I was young, I didn't see the impending danger coming. Before I knew what was happening, I was overwhelmed and have been trapped ever since. Thus I'm a prisoner, although a very knowledgeable one. I'll give you more details later, but I'm sure you'd first like me to tell you about some of the things I've seen during my long lifetime. Do feel free to send in your questions during this broadcast, and I'll do my best to answer them as I go along.

I was born toward the end of what you call the Eocene epoch. There was a large variety of animals in the forest where I lived, although some of the species you see today had not yet evolved. Because of my diminutive stature, I had to remain very careful not to be accidentally damaged or even deliberately eaten. My favourite companions were the monkeys. They were only small in those days, but were always playful, except when danger beckoned; then they made an awful noise. What's this – a question already? 'Did I see any dinosaurs?'

I don't think you must know much about palaeontology. Those big land-based beasts had been wiped out twenty-five million years before I came along. But there were many species of birds, some of which may have descended from those dinos you obviously love to hear about. Sorry to disappoint you on that score.

The life around me that I was observing, but not able to participate in due to my incarceration, seemed as if it would continue that way for ever. The time that I was born was the warmest it had been for millions of years. You talk a lot today about climate change and the need to reduce the carbon dioxide level. I can tell you that in my day it was massively high, which is what enabled the tropical trees and flowers around me to exist in great numbers.

However, I started to become aware that it was gradually becoming colder. It was explained to me many years later that Antarctica and Australia had originally been joined but were now separating. The same continental drifting was also occurring in the north. These movements changed the ocean currents and led to global cooling. Carbon dioxide levels dropped steeply, polar icecaps formed and sea levels fell. Some people even think the Earth had also been hit by asteroids.

Maybe you see this climate change as not being good for the planet. Sadly, many of the plant and animal species I'd come to know could not survive the cold and were wiped out. But it did turn out to be an advantage for me. If it hadn't happened, I probably wouldn't be here telling you all this. I'm also proud to report that my own species had obviously reached the peak of evolution because we are much the same now as we were those forty million years ago.

But I see another question has just come in: 'Did I see any cave men in those early days?'

Oh dear, that's about as far out as the question about dinosaurs. No, your earliest ancestors – the *Australopithecines* – came on the scene only about four million yeas ago, that's only a tenth of the time I've been here. The first modern humans like you have been around for less than a million years.

If there are no more questions for the moment, let me continue telling you about the changes I've seen. Eventually the Earth started to warm up again, but this respite was not permanent and before long the cold returned once more. This cycle of temperature ups and downs has continued to this day. Even in the last half a million years there've been five periods where the glaciers have formed and then receded. We are in the middle of a warm spell now, but it may not last. Come back in another hundred-thousand years and you may need your thermal underwear.

As an observer whilst all these climate changes were occurring, it was fascinating to see evolution at work. Although many animals I'd come to know had disappeared, with each of these cycles new species came along to replace them. Some of them soon became recognisable as early forms of those we see today. Had you been there you would have seen horses, cattle, pigs and deer, although they were still quite small compared with today's beasts.

No doubt you'll be especially interested to know that the earliest versions of your own ancestors, the great apes, arrived on the scene about twenty million years ago. However, it was another ten million before those of humans and chimpanzees separated, and they still had a long way to go before you could have recognised them as such.

But I must tell you something else that may surprise you. Did you realise it was only five million years ago that what was the Mediterranean Basin flooded and became a sea? We tend to think that features like seas and continents have always been the way they are today, but I can assure you that many are quite recent in the life of this planet.

Well, that's just a quick trawl through some of the things that have happened during my forty million years, so I'm ready for more questions now. Yes, I see someone asks how I can know so much about things that have happened far away from where I was incarcerated.

Yes, that's a good one, and the answer is that I may look dead in my present state but I'm very much alive. I can hear what people tell me and I can talk back to them just as I am doing now during this broadcast. You may think you can hear me through your ears, but that's just an illusion. My words are being projected directly into your mind, and you perceive them in your own language. Quite a clever trick, I'm sure you'll agree.

Ah, another two questions have just come in. The first asks me to explain how I became trapped, and the second refers to my earlier statement that I probably wouldn't be here today if global cooling had not occurred when it did. These are really two parts of one bigger question: 'what happened to me?' I think it'll be best if I start at the beginning.

I was happily feeding along with my friends on the bark of a conifer tree – actually I believe the name the boffins use for it is a *Sciadopity*. Anyway, the warning came time too late. Whereas my friends managed to fly away, I was caught in a ball of sticky resin rolling down the tree trunk. I struggled to free myself, but to no avail. This golden lump came to a halt before it reached the ground, and became my permanent home from that moment on.

My prison remained where it was for many years until eventually the glacier reached it. The powerful wall of ice easily demolished my tree and all the others in the forest, and I was enveloped by it. Spending such a long time frozen had the effect of hardening the resin around me. This made it less likely to be damaged, or eaten by some creature that was not particular about its diet. Eventually the glacier retreated back into the sea, taking me with it, and my capsule was at the mercy of the waves.

The time came when, as a smooth and glowing piece of amber, I was washed up onto the shores of the Baltic Sea in Poland. People collect stones like mine and make them into items of attractive jewellery. One day I was found and then sold to a collector of fossils.

I see another question: 'Was my piece of amber made into a fashion accessory?'

No, the collector keeps me in a transparent box on the shelf in his study. Thus, even as a humble Fungus Gnat, I can still look out on the world and observe the changes that occur over millennia, whereas you dear listener will only be able to witness a tiny fraction of this. Aren't you envious of me?

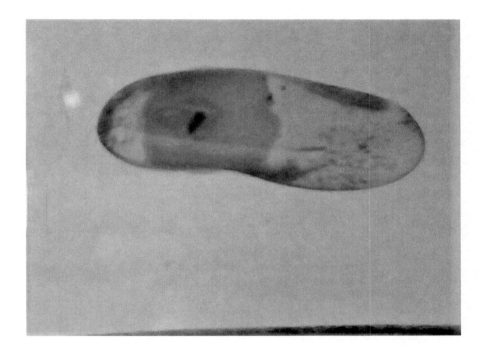

A piece of amber with an embedded insect. Author's image

Your House is on Fire

A year or so ago there was a television series that made me think. I can't remember the title, but it involved volunteers living in different houses and temporally having everything taken away from them. When I say 'everything', I mean *everything*.

Firstly, all the furnishings were removed from the house, including the contents of the draws, cupboards and wardrobes. Then the curtains were taken down. All that was left was the clothing that the individuals wore. Believe it or not, they then had to completely disrobe so that both they, and the house, were literarily stripped to the bone. All their belongings were locked up in a container several hundred yards away, but they were given the key.

Whilst this may sound like just an excuse for some tabloid voyeurism, it was filmed quite discretely and the objective was much more interesting. Each day, the volunteers were allowed to collect just a single item each from the locked container. On the first day, there was the inevitable fun and games of the men and women running on public footpaths to retrieve one of their belongings. To preserve their modesty, anything was grabbed, such as a discarded newspaper or a cardboard box from a neighbour's dustbin.

The point I'm leading up to is: if it were you, what would be the first and only possession you would take from the container? As might be expected, in most cases for the contestants it was an item of clothing to cover up their nakedness. But that left them without shoes, blankets, curtains, cooking utensils, cutlery, tools, mobile telephones, and even money to buy food to supplement the small supply of iron rations left for them.

As each day arrived, another item could be taken so that, after about a week (which might have been the limit of the experiment), the participants had acquired sufficient items to survive in relative comfort. They were all very brave to agree to this adventure, and I hope they were well compensated for it.

I thought a lot about what I would collect, especially on that first day. It obviously needed a strategy. Just grabbing at a pair of trousers, a workman's overall or similar onesie type of garment, might save some embarrassment, but it would leave you without anything else to wear or use around the house for another twenty-four hours. Would there be something you might take that had multiple uses, or from which other items could be made? Think about it for a moment before reading on.

One young lady, who was apparently living on her own, had a brilliant solution. She must have planned ahead, and had included a bale of cotton cloth among her possessions. This was the item she collected on that first day. There were many yards of material, so she just wrapped some of it around herself and calmly walked back to her house, carrying the remainder. Yes, it was just a single item, as specified by the rules, but it had many uses.

We saw her using a sharp screw sticking out of the wall where a fitting had been removed, to help her tear off strips of the material. She used some of these to tie around herself to make simple but adequate items of clothing, and also on her feet to act as slippers. Then she hung pieces up at the window to form temporary curtains. Perhaps there were also other uses including a towel or a bed sheet. It was clear that this participant far outshone all the others with her enterprise and adaptability.

Thus, the lesson to be learned was, don't just grab an item with just a single use, no matter how important it seems to be, instead select something that can be adapted to serve many functions. But would this also apply to the decision on what you would save if your house was on fire?

Of course we hope this will never happen to us, but should we nevertheless still have a contingency plan for this one-in-a-million eventuality? Let's assume there are no other inhabitants or pets to worry about, and just focus on possessions. Unlike the enterprising woman in the TV programme, our first choice would probably not be a bale of cloth. Even an item of clothing would be low down the list of priorities, unless we have just emerged from the shower or are awakened by the smell of burning during in the middle of winter.

As a precaution against such an eventuality, some people have a fire-proof box or cabinet to store essential documents like passports, house deeds, financial papers, and even some valuables. The hope is that, even if the house were to burn to the ground, the container would then be found among the rubble. This seems to be a good idea, because scrabbling around in filing cabinets trying to find those all-important papers whilst the room is burning around you might be hazardous for your health.

Hopefully we would be fully covered by fire insurance (the certificate safely stored in the fireproof box?), but that would not compensate for items of low intrinsic but high sentimental value. I asked a few friends what they would grab first, and treasured old family photographs were mentioned more than once. They would be worth nothing in the market place, unless you were a very famous individual. Then that item of jewellery that used to belong to your mother? Not valuable when compared with that gold watch given to you for your birthday, but priceless with regard to the memories it brings back to you of a departed loved one.

Some of those I asked did mention possessions that were special to them, and which were probably also valuable. One lady pointed to three original paintings, and another had had a collection of ceramic figures that she loved. In both cases these artworks gave great pleasure, and would be sorely missed if they fell victim to the flames.

The importance of documents relating to legal and monetary matters has already been mentioned but, with patience and persistence when fighting the bureaucratic system, most if not all, can probably eventually be replaced. Likewise, if you are of an academic persuasion and have amassed a collection of diplomas and certificates of which you are proud, losing them in the conflagration will be painful, although copies would usually be available.

What if you are a musician, and have one or more instruments that took a long time to find, and may even be quite rare? One lady I asked had a guitar that she loved playing, so she would make a big effort to save this before fleeing the house. I too have several instruments, and would be sad to see them go up in smoke. Money from the insurance would enable you to buy replacements, but would they be as good as the ones you have nurtured and cared for over the years? Perhaps the effort of going to all that trouble to find new ones might discourage you from playing again.

Surprisingly perhaps, only one person mentioned medication. Of course not everyone is taking prescribed potions but those who do will belong to one of two groups. You may be suffering from an acute ailment and need to take medicine for a limited period of time. It could be extremely risky not to complete the course, but have you recently tried to obtain a same-day appointment with your family doctor? My local GP surgery is probably not untypical in prominently displaying this: '72 hours notice is required for all repeat prescriptions.' Such a wait might have undesirable consequences for your health.

The other group comprise the many who have a daily pill-popping regime because of chronic conditions. Being one of those enjoying the third age of life, whilst I consider myself relatively fit, my breakfast every morning would not be complete without availing myself of the contents of the nest of little boxes inscribed with days of the week. Yes, they will all be replaceable, but why not just grab them on your way to the fire escape.

Another essential that was not mentioned as often as I had anticipated was your purse or wallet. Whilst the loss of a few coins or banknotes might not be so serious, in this day and age not having your debit or credit cards certainly is. Replacing these can take even longer than obtaining a repeat prescription, the more so if you've also lost your means of identification. Could you manage without cash in the meantime?

We live in the age of computers. Whilst some believe that, as they have managed without them for all these years, they don't need one now, the majority of us have embraced these infernal machines. Perhaps we just send the occasional email, or maybe we use them for research, internet buying, or writing whole books.

But, if it is vital that our work be saved for future reference, where do we store it? If only on the computer's memory, you will lose it if the machine is destroyed. For those clued-up in these things, there are a number of offline storage options, but you can also keep copies on a memory stick or portable hard drive. If the latter, would you want to grab these as you make a hasty retreat? If you have a laptop, would this be the first object you would save?

This brings me to the most obvious thing to pocket as you leave the building. Just like the enterprising woman who took a bale of cloth as her first possession, and cleverly found many uses for it, the same principle surely applies when your house is on fire. Maybe it depends on your age group. I asked mainly older folk, and they did not nominate what is probably the most useful single object to take, but younger boys and girls surely would.

Have you guessed what it is? A smart phone! Those who walk around, shutting out the world around them with earphones plugging up their hearing organs, concentrating intently in seeing who has contacted them in the last two minutes, would need little else. These days, the mobile phone not only makes calls, but is also a camera, satnav, mini computer, music player, money transfer device, and no doubt other things that I wouldn't understand if anyone tried to explain them to me.

I'm sure that many people born during the last few decades would feel just as naked without their phones as the contestants in the television series did without their clothes. All it needs is someone to invent an application that can be installed in these mobile gadgets that generates a cloak of invisibility for selected parts of the body, and then even a bale of cloth would be surplus to requirements. As for me – I shall just grab my pills, wallet, and memory sticks, and hope that it's not raining outside.

The Crystal Skull

"Are you sure those crystal skulls were made only a hundred or so years ago?" Scarlett asked her husband as the tourist coach from Mérida Airport approached Valladolid, their holiday destination on the Mexican Peninsula.

"There are many myths and legends associated with these fascinating objects," Hudson replied. "But all the research that's been carried out on them indicates they were carved using tools and abrasives that didn't exist in pre-Columbian times."

"What a shame," she said, shaking back her flaming hair. "I was so sure they were created by aliens who visited Chichen Itza or some other Aztec location a thousand years back. They'd have had equipment far superior to ours."

"Not only that," Hudson continued, avoiding comment on the alien theory, "the experts don't even believe the skulls were made in Central America. It's most likely they were carved in Germany from quartz imported from Brazil."

Quinn had been listening without comment up to this point. "I agree with Scarlett," he said. "One of the reasons the four of us came on this trip to Mexico was to absorb ourselves in the folklore and mythology of the Aztecs, and I certainly thought the crystal skulls were a part of this. Don't you agree Pandora?"

His fiancée nodded. "Well, that was one of the reasons but not the only one. This is a fascinating place, and there's much more pre-Columbian history to explore."

"Yes, and I just can't wait to have a chance to swim in one of the amazing cenotes," Hudson said. "Some of those water-filled sinkholes and their side caves are so deep that divers have yet to fully explore them. Who knows, there may be wonderful artefacts hidden there waiting to be discovered."

"So long as they don't include the bodies of those who were thrown into the pools as human sacrifices," Pandora commented, her face temporarily losing its habitual smile. "I've been reading up on them. The ancient Maya used the cenotes for water supplies, but don't ask me to drink out of them!"

"Always the health conscious one," Quinn said, laughing. "You've missed out on lots of treats because of your list of things you don't eat or drink, but I still love you."

"After nearly two hours on this coach I'm glad we look to be arriving at our hotel. I just can't wait to unpack and freshen up," Hudson said. "Let's all meet at the bar before dinner and we can discuss our plans for tomorrow."

"Well, I was expecting the food to be over-spiced but those shredded-beef tacos were delicious," Scarlett said pushing her empty plate away.

"And my corn on the cob elotes were something different, smothered with cheese, chilli and cilantro," Pandora commented, with one of those satisfied expressions that only come when one's middle regions are comfortably replete.

"Yes, no complaints with the grub," Hudson agreed. "But tomorrow's going to be exciting. Chichen Itza is one of the new Seven Wonders of the World. It was built by the Maya people about a thousand years ago and it's their largest pre-Columbian city."

"I believe there are many ruins as well as a hundred-foot high structure that's referred to as a pyramid, but it has four sides not three as the Egyptian ones have," said Quinn.

"And just like those in Egypt, I believe they're aligned to the points of the compass," Hudson added. "I wonder why."

"We were discussing crystal skulls on our way here," Quinn continued. "I read that the walls and panels at Chichen Itza contain hundreds of skulls carved in stone, not unlike the crystal models."

"Maybe they just represent all those who were thrown into the cenote as sacrifices," Hudson suggested.

"Oh dear we're back to all the dead bodies that could be at the bottom of the pool again," Pandora said with a shudder.

Quinn laughed. "Perhaps those carvings gave someone the idea of creating the crystal versions and then claiming they were ancient artefacts. If that's the case, they probably made a stack of money when they sold them."

"Yes. I did read that one went for the equivalent of 18,000 dollars in today's money," Hudson commented.

"Well, I still like to think there's more to them than modern creations," said Scarlett. "Perhaps one day there'll be a discovery that'll show some mystical power was involved."

"Are you still thinking that little green men landed and left them here when nobody was looking?" Pandora asked, trying to make it sound serious.

Scarlett's face took on a pained expression. "No need to make fun of my ideas. It's just that I read somewhere that paranormal claims have been made for them."

"Sorry, I didn't mean to be sarcastic. Do tell us more about these."

"Okay. Some believe they can produce miracles, cause visions, and even cure disease. Others think they contain the souls of ancient Mayans. And yes, there is indeed a belief that they're linked with life on Mars – the little green men you mentioned."

"Interesting," Pandora said. "Have there been any studies by scientists into these claims?"

"I've not heard of any support for them, so we'll just have to use our imagination."

The two men had been listening to these exchanges without commenting, but Hudson now spoke up. "Fascinating stuff, but it's been a long day and it's getting late. We've another coach journey tomorrow to reach Chichen Itza, so perhaps we should turn in now and enjoy a night's sleep."

* * *

"Wow!" exclaimed Scarlett. "I know we've seen pictures but now we're actually looking at it for real, that pyramid is just amazing. It reaches right up into the sky."

"Yes, its top does seem much higher then the one hundred feet you said it was," Pandora remarked, turning to her husband. "Can we go inside?

"Unfortunately not," said Hudson. "We can't even climb the outside now, as the authorities have fenced the whole thing off to stop vandalism. But there's a lot to see here so let's have a walk around the whole site."

"Ah, here's the stones with skulls carved into them, just as you mentioned," Pandora said as they came to the ruined walls. "I can't stop thinking about them representing those who were sacrificed by being thrown into the pool."

"I see you've also brought your swimming gear with you" Hudson said to Quinn. "It's getting quite hot so, if you're ready, I'd love to cool off in the cenote."

"Suits me," Quinn replied. "Are you ladies not going to join us for a dip in the pool?"

"Not for me, as you know," Scarlett said. "How about you Pandora?"

"No thanks. It looks to be a slippery walk down, and I still don't like the thought of what might be lurking in the water."

"Understood. Whilst Quinn and I go into the changing room, why don't you ladies sit down, have a cold drink and then look round the souvenir shop. We'll join you there when we've finished."

"That tonic water with lime was very refreshing on a hot day like this," Scarlet said.

Pandora nodded. "Before we go to the souvenir shop, let's go to the edge of the cenote and see if we can spot our men in the water."

"It certainly is pretty," Scarlett commented. "And those streamers from the trees at the top stretching right down into the pool just add to the magic."

"I agree. But there's quite a few people in the pool and I'm not sure if I could recognise anyone at this distance. No doubt our guys are enjoying themselves, so let's leave them to it and see if there's anything worth buying in the shop."

"Just the usual tourist stuff: fridge magnets, models of the pyramid, polo shirts and post cards," Pandora said half an hour later.

"Our men haven't arrived back yet, so let's keep looking; there's still one room we haven't been in yet."

Five minutes later Scarlett let out a shout: "Now here's something I *do* want to buy."

"What have you found there?"

"Small models of the crystal skulls. I just have to have one of those."

Pandora gave a laugh. "Do you think they'll have those mystical powers you've been reading about?"

"If I don't buy one, we'll never find out, will we?"

Scarlett selected one the quartz replicas and went to the check-out to pay for it. As she was waiting her turn the two men came into the shop. "Well, well," said Hudson, looking at the small object that his wife was holding in her hand. "I might have guessed you'd want to have one of those if you saw them. I hope they're not expensive."

"No," she replied defiantly. "But I'd still buy one if they were."

"Ah well, I'm sure we're going to be haunted from now on," he said with a laugh. "But let's sit down outside and we can tell you how wonderful it was to swim and snorkel in the cenote."

They chatted away, this time enjoying a cup of iced coffee, but Scarlett wasn't listening closely. Whilst the men told them about the beautifully clear water and the caves leading off from the main pool, her mind was already fanaticising about what the skull might have in store for her.

* * *

When Scarlett was alone, back at their hotel in Valladolid, she took the crystal skull out of its wrapping. 'Pity it's only an inch high,' she murmured to herself. 'I'd love to have one of the full-

sized ones, but this one looks just the same but on a miniature scale.' She examined the big round eye sockets, and then the full set of flawless teeth in the prominent jaw. 'Cleverly done, and it must have been carved because you can't melt quartz and put it in a mould.' Gazing at it intensely, she wondered if it had a story to tell, just like its big brothers.

"Scarlett. Scarlett. Have you been hypnotised by that thing?"

"Oh, hello Hudson. Sorry, I was just lost in thought about these skulls."

"I came in a couple of minutes ago but you were transfixed and didn't answer me. It's obvious it's put an evil spell on you."

Scarlett laughed, but did wonder if the little skull had somehow affected her mind. But perhaps not, we all experience these moments when we're lost in thought and oblivious to distractions. "Don't worry, darling. Haven't you ever been concentrating hard on something and not heard when somebody spoke to you?"

"Okay, I'll give you the benefit of the doubt this time. But shouldn't you be getting changed for dinner? Pandora and Quinn will be waiting for us in the bar any time now."

Dinner was as enjoyable as the one they had the previous evening. Scarlett did her best to join in the chit-chat about what they'd seen and done that day, but her mind kept drifting back to the souvenir she'd bought. Yes, there were a few jokey comments made by the others, but to her there was definitely something mystical about it.

Eventually they decided they'd eaten and drunk enough, and it had been another tiring day. The welcome of a comfortable bed beckoned.

Scarlett put her prized possession on the bedside table and tried to get some sleep. It didn't come easily. There was just enough light coming through the curtained window to enable her to see the little skull, and she kept opening her eyes to look at it. I'm sure it's trying to speak to me; its jaws seem to be moving, she mused. But that's impossible; it's just a solid lump of quartz.

She turned on her back to avoid seeing it and told herself to put these silly ideas out of her mind and try to sleep. But now she heard a voice – or did she just sense it? – that must be coming from the skull.

"I am trying to warn you," it seemed to say. Should she try to answer back? It all seems so silly as I'm sure it's just my imagination. Alright, I'll play along and see what happens. But I don't want to wake Hudson by speaking out loud. Silently, she mouthed, "Crystal skull, what is it you wish to warn me about?"

To her great surprise, she clearly heard the words: "A disaster will shortly happen here. You must leave this place as soon as you are able."

Surely this is all in my imagination, she tried to tell herself. But I'll play along with it for the moment. Mentally projecting her message she said, "What sort of disaster will this be, and when will it happen?"

She listened carefully but heard nothing. Trying just once more she muttered under her breath, "Can you give me more information?"

Still no response. She turned her head to look at the skull. Maybe the light through the curtains had faded in the last few minutes, as all she saw was an inert piece of carved rock. Obviously my mind has become obsessed with all these stories about the skulls; I must stick to logic and common sense from now on.

Her eyes closed and welcome slumber soon followed.

"Ah, that was a good night's sleep," Hudson said stretching himself. "How about you, darling?"

"Yes, we needed that after all we did yesterday. "But . . .". Scarlett hesitated, wondering if she had been about to make herself look foolish.

"But what?" Hudson asked. "Don't be afraid to tell me if you're worried about something."

"Okay, but don't laugh."

"Promise I won't."

"I'm sure I heard the skull talking to me. You said you wouldn't laugh, but I can see from your face you're about to."

"No, sorry," Hudson said, making an effort to contain himself. "It was an automatic reaction. Just tell me what you think you heard it say."

"You just said 'think' so you obviously won't believe me when I tell you. It said that we must leave this place because a disaster is about to happen."

Hudson now became more serious. "Did the skull say what sort of disaster it would be?"

"No, I asked it but there were no more communications."

"I've heard stories about the full-size skulls having premonitions, including one foretelling the assassination of President Kennedy but most people, including me, don't believe it."

Scarlett was pleased their discussion was taking a more serious direction. "Perhaps when we meet Pandora and Quinn this morning we can chat about this – after they've stopped laughing, that is."

"You have to admit it does sound like a tall story," Quinn said when they met up for coffee after breakfast. "I'd also read about people claiming that the skulls made such prophesies. Maybe their little relatives have inherited this ability."

"I don't want to dismiss this out of hand," Pandora said sympathetically. "Of course it may just be Scarlett's imagination, but there's lots about these parapsychology claims that science can't explain – at least not yet, and that includes these skulls."

"Thanks Pandora, it's nice to get a bit of understanding around here for a change," Scarlett replied. "Please share what you know about them. Hudson has already told me about the Kennedy assassination example."

"Well, I've read about their healing powers including curing cancer. On the other hand there's an example of one of them causing the death of a man."

"Impressive, if they're true, commented Quinn. "Anything else?"

"Only a general mention of them revealing ancient knowledge. Whilst all these could just be poppycock, it might be an idea not to simply dismiss them out of hand," Pandora said.

"What do you suggest we do now?" Scarlett asked.

"I think firstly we should see if there are any potential dangers around here, such as sink holes, earthquakes, fires or floods."

"Good idea. Let's ask some of the locals after we've finished coffee."

Hudson had remained silent up to now, but turned to face Scarlett. "Sorry love. I must admit that, at first, I thought you must have eaten some of those magic mushrooms. I'm still far from convinced we've anything serious to concern us, but it won't do any harm to check things out as you suggest. Also, I can't believe I'm saying this, but maybe you could try and talk to your little friend again tonight."

"We've nothing to lose by making a few enquiries," Quinn commented. "We're only here another two days before we have to take the bus to Mérida Airport and fly back to Mexico City for the rest of our holiday."

"Well, we've asked a couple shop keepers as well as our receptionist, but so far no one has warned us of any pending doom and gloom," Hudson said as they were enjoying a cooling drink at a road-side café. "We've spent most of the day exploring what Valladolid had to offer. Any suggestions?"

"We could always leave tomorrow, a day early, even if we don't take the skull's warning seriously," Scarlett commented. "We've probably seen most of what there is around here but nothing yet of Mexico City."

Pandora and Quinn agreed. "Okay, I'll go to the travel agent and change the plane tickets," Hudson said. "Shall we take the morning flight rather than the afternoon one? Right; so that's agreed. If you three want to call at the bus station to book our seats on the shuttle coach and then notify the hotel that we'll be leaving a day early, that'll take care of the formalities."

Back at the hotel, there was little more to do than pack their cases and meet up for their final dinner. "I must say I'm becoming a fan of these

Mexican delicacies," Pandora said, finishing the last of her garlic king prawn fajita.

Quinn gave a laugh. "Well, there'll be many more meals like this when we're in Mexico City, darling."

"Are you going to keep me awake talking to that skull tonight?" Hudson said to his wife.

"Now then, no need for sarcasm. If it wants to talk to me again, it will do so silently, and it'll be the same if I want to speak with it," she replied. "In fact, I might ask it for more details of this so-called pending disaster, just in case it responds."

The conversation reverted to more general matters about what they had already seen and what the capital city had in store for them. Eventually it was time to turn in. Scarlett again placed her souvenir on the bedside table and looked at it in the dim light. "Little skull, we have heard your warning and acted on it," she silently mouthed. "Please tell me more about this disaster."

She didn't expect a reply, but closed her eyes to try and sleep. Then words clearly entered her mind. "You have done well to heed my warning. A disaster will soon strike this place."

Trying to remain calm, she projected the question: "Again I ask you what this will be?" But, as it was the previous night, the communication ended and a welcome sleep ensued.

* * *

The announcement came over the public address system: "Please fasten your seat belts; we shall shortly be ready for take-off."

The aircraft gathered speed down the runway, lifted off the ground but then the starboard wing dipped alarmingly. Spontaneously shrieks came from the mouths of some of the passengers.

After a few moments the pilot managed to correct this and the plane continued its climb. "Whew! I was worried there for a moment," Pandora said. "I thought we were going to crash into the airport buildings."

Before the others had chance to comment, the loud speaker intervened again. "Ladies and gentlemen, this is your captain. Sorry about that incident; there was a strong gust of side wind that we didn't anticipate."

"You'd think the met office would've known this could happen," Quinn remarked.

But the captain had not finished. "A message has come from the control tower telling us there's been a rapid deterioration in the weather. Storm Victor, which was forming off the east coast, has unexpectedly increased in intensity. It looks like a hurricane is about to make landfall. All further flights to and from Mérida have been cancelled until further notice. Please keep your seat belts fastened for the duration of the flight, as we might encounter turbulence along the way."

"Oh dear," Scarlett moaned from the seat in front of their two companions. "I hope I don't become air sick if this happens; it doesn't take much to upset my stomach."

"I'm sure you'll be fine," Hudson assured his wife. "It was difficult to take seriously what you told us about the skull, but now it appears its warning was justified. If we'd stayed in Valladolid we'd have been marooned there and exposed to the full force of the storm."

"Of course you're right; it didn't immediately come into my mind. And it wasn't even essential to take the morning flight out; we could easily have decided to explore a bit more and leave in the afternoon. I'll have to thank my little crystal friend when this is all over."

The aircraft suddenly started shaking. Again there were spontaneous gasps from the passengers, but then all was steady again.

Another announcement from the captain quickly followed. "Ladies and gentlemen, Storm Victor appears to be heading westwards unusually quickly. I shall try to climb above the weather, or see if there is a calmer route to Mexico City. If the situation changes I'll let you know, but please stay in your seats. That also applies to the cabin crew so unfortunately no refreshments can be served at this time."

"We've nearly two hours on this flight, longer if the storm interferes," Hudson said. "The main thing is that we arrive safely, even if we're late."

A few minutes of calmness followed but then the plane started to veer violently off course, the force of the wind overpowering that of the engines. From the seats immediately behind them, Pandora was unable to suppress her panic. "We're going down; we're going to crash. I just know it!"

Quinn put his arm around her as far as the constraining seat belt would permit, and tried to sound convincing. "Of course we're not going to crash. These modern aircraft are built to withstand buffeting like this."

The pilot eventually managed to return the plane to its intended course and then climb to reclaim the height it had lost. "Apologies for that," he announced. "But pleased be prepared for similar incidents. We're in continuous contact with ground control, and they'll advise if it's necessary to divert to a different airport."

There was nothing more the passengers could do. Fate was not in their hands.

"I'm glad we managed to obtain a seat next to one of the emergency exits," Hudson said during a spell of calmness.

"What a thought," Scarlett replied. "Are you anticipating a crash landing where we'll have to be evacuated quickly before the plane explodes?"

"Well, one never knows. But we'd be among the first to get out."

"It's being so cheerful that keeps you going," his wife joked.

"Did you pack the crystal skull in your suit case?"

"Actually no. It's only small and I have it here in my handbag."

"Perhaps you should take it out and see if it wants to give you another message," Hudson said.

Scarlett adopted that pained look. "Are you being sarcastic again?"

Hudson showed no sign of levity. "No, but the warning it gave you last time did turn out to be justified. Whilst I'm not totally convinced it wasn't just a coincidence, let's give it another opportunity to communicate."

Scarlett took the skull out of its padded bag, held it in the palm of her hand and stared at it. "Come on my little friend, do tell us what's in store for us," she said quietly. Did its mouth start to move, or did she imagine it? Puttering it to her ear she was sure it whispered, "A disaster will occur. . ."

Before it could say any more, if indeed it had intended to do so, the aircraft was again caught in a powerful wind and started plummeting earthwards. The skull fell out of Scarlett's hand and rolled out of sight on the floor. "Don't worry about it," Hudson said. "We can look for it later."

All the passengers could do was hold tight and hope the pilot would be able to quickly return the plane to its intended course. But that did not happen.

"Ladies and gentlemen," a breathless captain announced. "The storm has now been rated as a hurricane. We will have to make an emergency landing. Control has just advised us that we have been cleared to land at a military airbase only a short distance away. There is likely to be considerable buffeting, but please remain calm whilst we make our approach."

In contrast to the earlier shrieking, there was now an eerie silence as the passengers prepared themselves for whatever fate had in store, and the pious ones quietly prayed that they would survive.

Hudson held Scarlett's hand and whispered, "Did the skull tell you anything?"

"I'm sure it started to say something about a disaster, before I dropped it. I'm frightened."

He squeezed her hand tightly. "Don't worry darling; we'll get through this. I bet that's what your little friend was trying to say." The conversation ended. Past life experiences started to flash through their minds.

The plane continued its downward spiral, and those brave enough to look out of the window through the streaming rain could see the wings shaking up and down alarmingly. Although the pilot was valiantly doing his best to level out, the ground was becoming dangerously close. With a final effort, he managed to bring the nose up just as the runway lights appeared.

"I can't bear to look," Scarlett said. "Are we going to make it down safely?"

"I'm sure we will," Hudson replied, not altogether convincingly."

Just as the landing gear was about to make contact with the landing strip, a violent gust of wind started to flip the plane over on the side where they were sitting. The tip of the starboard wing hit the runway and the emergency exit door burst open. Baggage fell off the overhead lockers and tumbled out of the door.

The passengers could see sparks flashing past the windows as the pilot fought to straighten the aircraft. Mercifully he managed to do so. But the undercarriage collapsed and plane skidded along on its belly before eventually coming to a halt at the end of the runway.

A spontaneous cheer came from the passengers. Pandora sitting behind them shouted, "We're safe." But it was a little premature. The smell of burning wafted in through the open door.

"Cabin crew, open all the emergency doors and let the escape chutes deploy. Then evacuate the passengers quickly. Leave all the luggage where it is." As they all slid down the chutes, they were relieved to hear the sirens of the airfield emergency vehicles arriving to tackle the fire that had started underneath the plane.

"Stand well clear of the aircraft," the fire chief shouted, once all the passengers and crew were safely outside. "The blaze is near the fuel tanks and they might explode at any moment."

His prediction was accurate. Moments later there was a mighty explosion and the plane was enveloped in flames. "We've lost all our baggage," Pandora cried.

Quinn put his arm around her, holding her tightly. "But we are safe, love. We can replace all our belongings, but we can't replace ourselves."

"I agree," Scarlett commented bravely. "Let's be positive about this; it's something exciting to tell the folks back home. But there's one thing I'm very sad about: I've lost my magical crystal skull."

"It's survived all these years, and I'm sure it's immortal," Hudson said. "Maybe it fell out of the aircraft when the emergency door burst open. It could be lying out there on the runway somewhere."

As the transport arrived to begin shuttling the passengers to the airfield buildings, Scarlett said, "Let's hope so. It did help us and I'm sure it'll do the same for whoever finds it. I'd love to go and look for it but doubt I'll be allowed to do so. Good bye, my little friend, and thank you."

END

Miniature crystal skull. Author's image.

A Covid Christmas Carol

"Bah! I just hate Christmas," Tom declared from behind his newspaper.

"What's up with you now, you old misery?" Mary responded, in a voice usually reserved for a winging child rather than a husband.

"It's Christmas Day tomorrow, and it's bad enough having to put up with all these silly decorations and spending money on cards and stamps. With the Covid lockdown we won't be able to meet our two sons, or even go out for a meal on our own. As for holidays, they're now just a distant memory."

"Cheer up," said Mary. "We've a lot to be thankful for – a warm house, food on the table. And we'll be able to see our family on the computer screen, thanks to modern technology. Just think of the poor, the homeless, and those living on the streets."

Tom remained firmly stuck in his melancholic bubble. "It's alright saying that, but we've worked hard to achieve what we have, without asking for any favours. We deserve these home comforts, but why did the dammed virus have to come along and spoil our plans like this."

"I know, and I feel bad about it too, but just think we should count our blessings. There's nothing we can do about it, and the situation will improve quickly once we've all been vaccinated. This isn't the first time we've had to make sacrifices for reasons out of our control."

"Well at my age I think I've put up with enough," Tom said sulkily. "I'm just cheesed off. There's nothing to watch on television, and tomorrow is going to be miserable. I'm going to bed, and just hope I'll only wake up when it's all over."

Mary knew that, once he was determined to feel sorry for himself, there would be no point in trying to shake him out his mood. "Alright, you go; I'll be up later. I'm sure you'll end up having a happy Christmas after all."

All she received in reply was a grunt.

Tom completed his ablutions and climbed into bed. Still feeling grumpy, and not a bit tired, he opened the book on his bedside table. But it was not long before his eyes started to close. He switched off the light and was soon asleep. It was only moments later, or so it seemed, when he sensed that someone had entered the room. No, it was't Mary, she was asleep beside him. It was the pale figure of a man.

"Who are you? How did you get in without me hearing you?" Tom shouted, his voice shaking.

"You have nothing to fear. I shall not harm you, and will be gone very soon."

Tom made a stalwart effort to remain calm. "What do you want with me?"

"I have come to talk to you about your past, to remind you of what you were like as a child," his visitor replied, sounding rather distant even though he was only a metre away.

"Why should I need to be reminded of those times; they're long gone and I'm now retired?"

"All in good time," the man replied. "You had a lonely childhood, and were sent to a boarding school, away from your family."

"How do you know all this? Are you proposing to blackmail me for things I might have said and done over half a century ago?"

His visitor again ignored the questions. "I told you there was nothing to fear. After you left school, you started work in a bank, determined to climb your way to the top. Two years later, you became engaged to Elizabeth."

Tom had now lost his fear, and was thinking back to his early days. "Ah yes, dear Elizabeth, but she eventually ended our relationship and married someone else."

"That is correct; she realised you were more interested in your career than in caring for her. Do you remember visiting her ten years later, and seeing how happy she was with her large family?"

"Yes, that could have been me with her if I hadn't been so preoccupied with money," Tom said in a melancholic voice, eyes lowered. When he looked up again, his visitor had disappeared. I must have been dreaming but it did bring back memories, he mused, as he drifted into a fitful sleep.

Once again he became aware somebody had entered the bedroom and was standing close to him. Thinking his visitor had returned he said, "So you've come back to continue your interrogation."

But it was not the same person. "I have come to talk to you about your life now," the figure said, sounding very much like his predecessor.

"I know what my life is like now," Tom retorted. "Just go away and leave me in peace."

His visitor persisted. "Do you know what others make of you?"

"Surprise me," Tom said, now deciding the joke had gone far enough.

"They see you as someone only motivated by money, and who cares nothing for those who need help. There are many in this world who struggle with illness and poverty. You never donate to charity, or buy food or clothing for those who struggle for even the basics of life."

"I've worked hard for what I have," Tom replied defensively. "Why should I hand out money to those who can't be bothered to put in an honest day's work? Too many people just expect the State to give them everything they need."

"Just one other thing before I leave you," the visitor said. "Your miserly attitude is not bringing you happiness; it is making you miserable because you always want more. This is how others see you – grumpy and an old scrooge." With that, he faded away.

What a load of nonsense, Tom thought, turning over in bed and doing his best to resume his slumbers.

"Oh no! Not another one," he shouted angrily at his third caller of the night. "What do *you* want?"

"I have come to tell you what the future holds."

"Okay, tell me, Mister Fortune Teller."

"Your wife has been loyally supportive over the years, but now doubts she can continue living with you. She is thinking about a divorce."

Tom laughed. "Pull the other one; I don't believe you."

"Your two sons feel relieved they won't have to put up with you at Christmas this year. They are sorry for their mother, and support her wish to be rid of you. You will die alone and unloved."

"What a load of lies," Tom said. "How do you know all this?" But his visitor had departed.

Tom woke up to the smell of breakfast floating up the stairs. He went down to the kitchen, gave Mary a big kiss and said with a wide grin, "Ho Ho Ho! Merry Christmas darling."

"And a Merry Christmas to you, Tom," she said, looking quizzically at him. You're very bright and cheerful this morning; are you ill?"

"No, but I did some thinking during the night. I hope I didn't disturb you with my ramblings."

"No, I didn't hear anything."

"Do we still have that festive jumper you bought me last year, which I never wore?"

Mary nodded. "Yes, I put it away intending to give it to charity, but forgot to take it."

"Good, I'd like to wear it when we meet the family on the video link. But after breakfast we must watch the traditional carol service on television. It's going to be a happy day."

"Well, I'm so glad to hear this, in view of your mood yesterday," Mary said.

"I'm so sorry to have been miserable like that, but I've now come to my senses," replied Tom.

"We're going to have fun from now on. I want to invite the boys to join us on a cruise around the Mediterranean once all the restrictions are lifted. It'll be wonderful for us all to be together."

I wonder what brought about this change in Tom, Mary pondered, but I'm delighted that, despite all the best efforts of Covid-19, his Christmas blues have finally gone.

(With acknowledgement to Charles Dickens)

* * * * * * * * * *

About The Author

Mike was born in Yorkshire, where he remained until he married Susan. The couple first moved to Cheshire and then, with their two children, spent twenty years in South Africa. On their return, now with a family increased by one, they settled in Northampton.

Convinced that he did not achieve much at school, Mike was motivated to seek further education whenever and wherever the opportunity presented itself. This has been responsible for an eclectic mix of jobs over the years, ranging from laboratory technician, microbiologist, quality manager, human resource officer, psychologist, and university lecturer.

His interest in writing was born from the many assignments and articles he penned during his studies. The first of his ten books to date (one being co-authored) was based on an academic dissertation, and four more non-fiction works followed. After a memoir about his time overseas, he embarked on three collections of short stories and two historical novels. However, much of Mike's pleasure comes from carrying out the research that underpins his narratives.

Mike has been an active musician for most of his life, buying his first instrument – an old clarinet – when he started work at the age of sixteen. Currently he plays in a swing quintet, a small church group, and leads the Northampton U3A Dixielanders.

My father worked as a journalist on a provincial evening newspaper and I'm sure he would have loved me to have entered the same profession. The folk in the office had a wicked sense of humour. My dad once told me that a group of journalists tried to create what would be the world's most sensational headline. Each time they met in the pub after work they managed to add a bit more, until they finally settled on:

Unfrocked bishop in sex-change mercy dash to Palace corgi

Despite the enjoyment of interacting with people whose profession involved the written word, my career ambition lay elsewhere. Although I published many academic papers, it was only on retirement that I turned to writing for the general reader. However, my stories are underpinned by a continued interest in research to ensure the factual aspects are as accurate as possible.

Printed in Great Britain
by Amazon

29020226R00106